This book is dedicated to my father, who will always be my number one hero. He spent twenty years on active duty defending our country, and he has spent a lifetime caring for and protecting his family He's what heroes are made of, and I love him so very much.

Love you, Dad!

Chapter One

Declan O'Neill hiked his rucksack higher on his shoulders and trudged down the sidewalk in downtown Washington, DC. The last time he'd seen so many people in one place, he'd been a fresh recruit at US Marine Corps Basic Training in San Diego, California, standing among a bunch of teenagers, just like him, being processed into the military.

He shouldered his way through the throngs of sightseers, businessmen and career women hurrying to the next building along the road. The sun shone on a bright spring day. Cherry blossoms exploded in fluffy, pinkish-white dripping petals onto the lawns and sidewalks in an optimistic display of hope.

Hope.

Declan snorted. Here he was, eleven years after joining the US Marine Corps…eleven years of knowing what was expected of him… of not having to decide what to wear each day. Eleven years of a steady paycheck, no matter how small, in an honorable profession, making a difference in the world.

Now he was faced with the daunting task of job hunting with a huge strike on his record.

But not today.

Why he'd decided to take the train from Bethesda, Maryland, to the political hub of the entire country was beyond his own comprehension. But with nowhere else to go and nothing holding him back—no job, no family, no home—he'd thought *why not?*

He'd never been to the White House, never stopped to admire the Declaration of Independence, drafted by the forefathers of his country, and he'd never stood at the foot of the Lincoln Memorial, in the shadow of the likeness of Abraham Lincoln, a leader who'd set the United States on a revolutionary course. He'd never been to the Vietnam War Memorial or any other memorial in DC.

Yeah. And so what?

Sightseeing wouldn't pay the bills. Out of the military, out of money and sporting a dishonorable discharge, Declan would be hardpressed to find a decent job. Who would hire a man whose only skills were superb marksmanship that allowed him to kill a man from four hundred yards away, expertise in hand-to-hand combat and the ability to navigate himself out of a paper bag with nothing more than the stars and his wits?

In the age of the internet, desk jobs and background checks, he was doomed to end up in a homeless shelter. With his last ninety-eight dollars and fifty-five cents burning a hole in the pocket of his rucksack, he'd decided to see the country's capital before he couldn't afford to. As for a place to sleep? He could duke it out with the other homeless people for a back alley or a park bench. Maybe he'd get lucky and someone would slit his throat and put him out of his misery.

He paused at a corner, waiting for the light to change and the little walking man to blink on in bright white.

As he waited, he noticed a couple of dark SUVs sandwiching a long, sleek white limousine. Not that he hadn't seen at least half a dozen limousines pass in the last twenty minutes he'd been walking. But he was standing still now and had nothing else but the backs of people's heads to stare at.

The lead SUV turned on the street in front of Declan.

Before the limousine could follow suit, a white van erupted from a side street, tires screaming, and plowed through the people traversing a crosswalk to cut off the white limousine before it could make the turn.

Another white van followed the first and raced to block the rear of the limousine, effectively bracketing the big vehicle.

Men dressed in dark suits and ties jumped out of each of the dark SUVs, weapons drawn. They'd only taken two steps when the sliding doors on the vans slashed open and men in dark clothes and ski masks leaped out, carrying submachine guns.

"Get down!" Declan yelled. He grabbed the blond-haired woman in the fancy skirt suit beside him and shoved her to the ground as bullets sprayed into the men in suits from the SUV. Declan threw his body over the woman's, shielding her from the rain of bullets.

The men and women surrounding him dropped to the pavement out of fear or injury. Ladies screamed, children cried and chaos reigned.

While the gunmen from the white van continued to fire toward the pedestrians, more men piled out of the vans and raced for the white limousine. They yanked at the vehicles' doors, but the handles didn't budge.

One of the attackers aimed at the handle and pulled the trigger on his handgun.

The limousine door burst open. A black-suited bodyguard poked a gun out and fired.

The man who'd shot the door handle edged out of range, jammed his handgun through the door and pulled the trigger.

Over the top of the other side of the vehicle, another man in a dark suit emerged from inside the limousine and aimed at the man who'd just shot one of the limousine passengers.

From his prone position, Declan watched as it all went down. Whoever the security detail was guarding must have been important enough for trained gunmen to stage such a daring operation in the middle of the day, on a crowded street.

Unable to stand by while people were being attacked, Declan shrugged out of his rucksack and shoved it toward the woman he'd pushed to the ground. "Watch this," he commanded. "I'll be back in a minute."

The woman lay with her cheek to the ground, her eyes wide, a frown marring her pretty features. "Where are you going?"

"I can't just stand by and do nothing." He bunched his legs beneath himself and pushed to a low crouch.

A hand reached up to capture his arm. "Don't. They'll kill you."

"If nobody does anything, they'll kill everyone in that limousine and the security detail that was supposed to protect them."

"But you're only one man." She stared up at him with soft gray eyes.

"Just watch my ruck. Everything I own is in that bag. And stay down." He didn't wait for her response. Instead, he ran to the side of a Lincoln Town Car that had stopped short of the vans and SUVs caught in the crossfire.

The driver lay sideways in his seat, the front windshield having been peppered with bullet holes. He wasn't moving, his eyes open, unseeing.

Declan moved on, keeping the body of the sedan between him and the men wielding submachine guns. He waited for the shooter closest to him to turn away before he pounced, throwing the man off-balance and pushing him to the ground. With a combination of surprise and strength, he took the man down and jerked his head back with a decided snap.

The man hadn't even fired another round. He lay still, unmoving at Declan's feet.

Declan retrieved the attacker's submachine gun and moved to the next man closest to him. Again, his attention focused on the limousine and the crowd lying crouched against the concrete sidewalks.

Moving silently, Declan eased up behind the next guy.

A scuffle with another security guard in the limousine generated more shouting and an eruption of gunfire.

Under the resulting confusion, Declan made his move and took out the next attacker, bringing him to the road surface with barely a whimper before he snapped his neck.

Sirens wailed in the distance.

One of the attackers yanked a dead security guard out of the back seat of the limousine and reached in to grab someone.

"Let go!" a voice inside yelled.

The attacker yanked a woman out of the limousine. She had gray hair and wore a dark gray suit and sensible pumps. "Don't hurt anyone else. I'll go with you. Just don't hurt anyone else."

He pulled her against him and pointed the handgun against her temple.

Declan cursed silently beneath his breath. A

hostage meant the attackers had more than the upper hand. No matter how many bad guys he took out, he couldn't get to the one who held the bargaining chip. Unless...

He'd worked his way closer to the white van blocking the front of the limousine. A couple of bad guys stood at the front of the vehicle and one guarded the rear.

Declan rolled beneath a long black sedan parked several feet away from the van. If he could just make it to the van the kidnapper was edging toward, he might be able to...

A police car rounded the corner two blocks away, lights flashing, siren screaming. It ground to a halt. The two officers inside flung open their doors and leaped out, using the doors as shields.

"Time to go," the kidnapper shouted. Holding his victim with the gun to her head, he hurried toward the van closest to Declan.

If the kidnapper made it inside, the police

would not be able to stop him without potential injury to the woman.

The van door slid open. A man inside grabbed the kidnapper's arm and the woman's and yanked them both inside.

The rest of the attackers backed toward the other van, still providing cover but unaware of Declan standing near the rear of the kidnapper's vehicle.

As the sliding door started to close, Declan reached for the back door of the van. The handle turned, the door swung open and Declan leaped in as the sliding side door slammed shut.

Four bad guys filled the interior. The kidnapper had released his charge and was in the process of shoving the woman to the floor of the van.

When she collapsed to her knees, Declan had a clear shot.

He braced himself and pulled the trigger on

the submachine gun as the driver shifted the gear into Reverse.

The kidnapper and the man who'd helped him into the vehicle dropped on top of the woman and lay still.

"Stop the vehicle," Declan yelled. "Or I'll shoot."

The man in the passenger seat swiveled, a handgun in the palm of his hand.

Declan didn't hesitate—he fired several shots at the man, the bullets hitting him in the arm and penetrating the back of the seat. The man slumped forward, the pistol falling from his hand.

The driver hit the accelerator, with the vehicle still in reverse, and he pulled hard on the steering wheel.

Centrifugal force flung Declan across the bed of the van. He hit the other side with his right shoulder, losing his hold on the submachine gun. The weapon clattered to the floor and skittered beyond his fingertips, out of Declan's reach.

As he righted himself, the driver shifted into Drive and gunned the engine.

Barely reclaiming his equilibrium, Declan staggered backward, caught himself and lunged for the driver, ready to end the rodeo. He grabbed the back of the driver's seat to brace himself and then wrapped his arm around the driver's throat and pulled up hard. "Park it. Now!" he yelled.

The driver clutched at the arm with one hand and steered with the other, directing the van toward a heavily populated sidewalk and the corner of a brick building beyond.

With a quick twist, Declan snapped the man's neck, shoved him to the side, leaned over the back of the seat and steered the van away from the crowded sidewalk and back into the street crowded with other vehicles.

Though dead, the driver's foot remained on the accelerator.

Declan held on tightly as the vehicle plowed into a delivery truck, rocking it on its wheels. The van crunched to a full stop, slinging Declan forward.

Because he held on to the back of the driver's seat, he wasn't thrown through the window; instead he flipped over the back of the seat, hit his head on the steering wheel and landed headfirst into the driver's seat.

He lay stunned for a moment, a dull pain throbbing in his head where he'd hit the steering wheel, but he was alive. He pushed backward over the seat, sat down hard on the floor of the van and surveyed the carnage.

A moan sounded from beneath the two men who'd hauled the woman inside.

Declan shook the gray haze from his head and crawled toward the groan. "Ma'am, are you okay?"

For a moment, nothing but silence came from beneath the two men.

"Ma'am?" Declan repeated. "Are you all right?"

"Can't breathe," her voice sounded.

Declan dragged the top man out of the way and then the other. Blood soaked the woman's gray suit, though she showed no signs of open wounds or ripped clothing. Declan assumed the blood wasn't hers. When she tried to sit up, he touched her shoulder. "You might want to lie still. You could have an injury from being handled so roughly."

"I'm all right…no broken bones… I just need to…sit up." She pushed to an upright position, her hands covered in the blood of her captors.

Declan glanced through the front windows.

Police vehicles surrounded the van, and men in SWAT uniforms rushed toward them, rifles aimed at the van.

"The police have arrived," he said.

"Thank God." The older woman wiped her hands on her skirt, leaving bright red streaks.

Then she pushed the gray hair back from her face and squared her shoulders, a frown pulling her brow downward. "Do you think they know these terrorists have been stopped?"

"We can't bank on it. They might take one look at me and shoot."

Her eyebrows shot upward. "But they can't. You saved my life."

"You in the van, come out with your hands up!" said a voice amplified by a bullhorn outside.

"Coming out," Declan said. "Don't shoot!" He reached for the door handle.

The gray-haired woman touched his arm. "Let me go first. Surely they won't shoot me, and I can let them know you're one of the good guys."

Declan shook his head. "You never know when one of them might get trigger-happy. I'll go first...with my hands up."

"At least let me open the door so they will see your hands up." The woman grabbed the handle and pulled back, opening the door slowly. "Don't shoot," she called out. "We're unarmed."

When Declan stepped out of the van, he held his hands high.

"On your knees!" a voice boomed.

Declan dropped to his knees.

"Hands behind your head."

Declan laced his hands behind his neck.

The man with the bullhorn called out, "Anyone else in the van, get out now, hands in the air."

Out of the corner of his eye, Declan could see the gray-haired woman step out of the van, her hands held high, her hair disheveled and blood smears on her gray suit.

"On your knees. Hands in the air," boomed the man with the bullhorn again.

"I will not go down on my knees in this skirt. Never mind, my knees can't take that kind of brutality." She started to drop her hands, but must have thought better of it and held them higher. "My kidnappers have been disabled and are in the van behind me." She nodded toward Declan. "This young man saved my life. I expect you to treat him well."

"Ma'am, you need to get on your knees," a SWAT officer said from behind the door of his vehicle.

Declan glared at the man. "She's not the problem."

"Silence," the SWAT guy said. "On your knees."

"Oh, for the love of Pete." The woman dropped her arms and eased herself to the ground, on her knees.

"Hands in the air," the SWAT team leader commanded.

"Pushy bastard, aren't you?" the woman said.

A chuckle rose up Declan's throat. He swallowed hard to keep from emitting the sound.

The SWAT leader motioned for his men to close in on the van. Once they ascertained the other men inside the vehicle weren't a threat, they dragged them out on the ground and laid them out in a line.

The other van had been stopped before it had gone two blocks. The men who'd been inside were lined up on their knees, being handcuffed.

Several SWAT team members approached Declan with their rifles pointing at Declan's chest.

He didn't dare move or breathe wrong. With a vanload of dead men, they would assume the worst first and check the facts later. Declan couldn't blame them. Not with the woman bathed in blood.

"I told you, this man saved my life," she was saying. "Treat him well, or I'll have your jobs."

"It's okay," Declan said quietly. "I'll be all right."

"You'd better be," she said with a frown. "I haven't had a chance to thank you properly."

A man grabbed his wrist and pulled his arm down behind his back. Then he pulled the other one down and bound them with a thin strand of plastic. Once they had him zip-tied, they yanked him to his feet and patted him down thoroughly, removing his wallet and dog tags. "Declan O'Neill, you'll have to come with us."

"Aren't you going to tell me why I'm being detained, and read me my Miranda rights?" Declan asked.

"We will. On the way to the station," the man closest to him said.

"I left my backpack with a bystander. I'd like to get it before we leave for the station."

Before Declan finished speaking, the SWAT team leader was shaking his head. "I'm sorry. But you'll have to come with us now."

"You don't understand." Declan stood still, resisting the pressure on his arm. "That back-pack is all I have in this world." Geez, he sounded like a pathetic homeless character. Then again, he was homeless.

The SWAT team leader nodded to one of his guys. "Find the man's backpack."

One of his men peeled out of the group and walked toward the bystanders on the sidewalk.

Forcibly dragged, Declan had no other choice but to go with the officers. He was shoved into the back seat of a police service vehicle, and then the door was shut in his face.

Without his backpack, he had nothing. Absolutely nothing. It contained his last bit of cash, a couple changes of clothing and photographs of him and his Force Recon team before they'd either been killed or split asunder. His phone was also in his backpack. It contained the numbers for his friends. He couldn't remember any of them off the top of his head. He'd never needed to commit the numbers to memory. They'd always been in his phone directory. Now he wished he had taken the time to learn the numbers.

His heart hurt as the vehicle pulled away. He twisted in the seat and stared back at the crowd, searching for the blond-haired woman. He didn't see her or his rucksack. The man who'd gone looking for it was on his way back to the rest of the SWAT team...empty-handed.

His only hope was if they gave him at least one call. He hoped the woman he'd left the rucksack with would answer the cell phone inside one of the pockets. And he prayed it had enough battery power left for her to answer. Considering he hadn't had a chance to charge the cell phone, he doubted it would ring.

Just when he'd thought he'd sunk as low as life could take him, he'd once again been proven wrong.

Chapter Two

Grace Lawrence had been on her way to interview for a job when the attack began and she'd been dragged to the ground and covered by the hulking hunk of a man. Too stunned to resist, she'd lain still, listening to the popping sound of shots being fired and the screams and shouts of women and men as they dove for cover.

All too soon, the man on top of her shifted and shoved his backpack at her, telling her to keep it safe. Left unprotected, she lay as flat to the ground as she could. Afraid of getting shot, Grace remained still for a few seconds after the man had left her with his camou-flage rucksack. Gunfire seemed to blast from all around her. Some women continued to scream or sob, while other people fled.

She lifted her head high enough to see an older woman being hauled out of the limousine and shoved toward a white van.

Her gaze scanned the area, searching for the stranger who'd left the rucksack with her. She'd seen him dart toward a vehicle and roll beneath the chassis. Then she'd lost sight of him.

Her heart raced as she considered what could be happening. The man could have left her with a bag full of explosives. She could be holding on to a bomb that was about to blow her and the entire block to hell and back.

She shoved the rucksack away from her, knowing it wouldn't be far enough. And she couldn't get up and move...not with bullets flying through the air. Then she spied Mr. Rucksack running from the front of one vehicle to the back of another, edging his way toward one of the men holding a submachine gun. What man would leave a bag full of explosives and then go after an armed shooter, barehanded?

As she watched, the hunky rucksack owner took down the gunman without being noticed, and then dragged the guy out of sight. The next moment, her guy's feet appeared beneath the carriage of another vehicle, heading toward the white van.

Was he out of his mind? There had to be a dozen gunmen scattered around the vans, limousine and security vehicles. How could one man stop all of those attackers?

Grace pulled the rucksack toward her and clutched it close to her chest. He'd asked her to watch his bag. Hell, he could end up dead before the attack was over. She might hold the only clue to his identity and be called upon to help identify his body.

A shiver ran through her. Grace sent a silent prayer to the heavens that the crazy man trying to stop a deadly attack didn't die that day. She didn't want to visit a morgue, and he was too good-looking to leave the world just yet. He deserved to live long enough to grow old and gray and develop a gut and wrinkles. Which would probably look good on him, as well.

When the sirens sounded in the distance, the group of attackers fired off rounds and backed toward the white vans. One of the men held the gray-haired woman at gunpoint, shoving her ahead of him. When they reached the van, the side door slid open and the man and woman were yanked inside.

Remaining attackers fired again and ran toward the second white van at the rear of the limousine.

The van with the woman inside backed away from the limousine and spun around.

At the same time as the side door slammed shut, the back door of the van swung closed.

But not before Grace saw who had climbed into the rear of the van.

Her breath caught and held. The man who'd saved her from being mowed down by the gunmen had entered the back of the van.

Had she been wrong? Was he with the bad guys after all? She glanced at the rucksack, afraid to move in case it would explode.

Then the white van veered erratically and gunfire sounded from inside.

"Get up and move!" someone yelled. A hand reached down and dragged Grace to her feet.

Despite her misgivings, she grabbed the rucksack and ran, stumbling away from the commotion.

Police cars and SUVs converged on the street, blocking the other white van. The one her guy was in drove up on a sidewalk.

People scattered.

The van swerved back out onto the road and crashed into a delivery truck, bringing it to a stop.

A police car arrived beside Grace and officers leaped out. One pulled his weapon and aimed at the white van, while the other waved his arms. "Move back. The show's not over."

Herded like cattle, Grace and the others caught in the attack were urged to run until they were a full two blocks away from the scene.

The crowd thinned enough that Grace was finally able to stop and turn around.

She waited with the rucksack clutched to her chest, the weight of the bag making her arms ache.

"Lady, move along," a police officer advised. "You don't want to get hit by stray bullets."

Beyond the police officers now blocking the sidewalk and street, Grace could see the white vans had been stopped. The men inside the one farthest away dropped to the ground, hands high in the air.

The other was still for what seemed like

a very long time before the door slid open and Mr. Rucksack stepped out and dropped to the ground on his knees. Shortly afterward, the gray-haired woman stepped out with her hands up.

That was him, her rucksack guy. Grace recognized his faded gray sweat jacket and short dark hair.

Grace took a step forward.

A police officer blocked her path. "Sorry, ma'am, I can't let you go in there."

"But, that man…"

The officer shook his head. "You'll have to stay back."

The SWAT team secured her guy's hands behind his back and led him to a waiting squad car. A moment later, it sped away.

Grace stared down at the rucksack. Now what was she supposed to do with it?

She found a bench and sat. Holding the bag between her feet, Grace waited for most of the people passing by to clear the area before she opened the bag. Then she drew in a deep breath and unzipped one of the sections. She told herself that if it exploded, she wouldn't know what happened. It would kill her instantly. Still, she couldn't help closing her eyes. When nothing happened, she opened them and searched through the interior of one compartment after another. Inside, she found a pair of worn jeans, a couple of T-shirts, several pairs of boxer shorts and a shaving kit. No plastic explosives, sticks of dynamite or detonators were hiding inside the bag.

She pulled out an envelope filled with photographs of men in marine uniforms, fully outfitted with weapons, helmets, rifles and ammunition. They stood in what appeared to be a camp in the desert.

The man who'd entrusted his rucksack with her was military or prior-military. No wonder he'd taken on the attackers like he knew what he was doing.

Her heart squeezed hard in her chest. And

the police had treated him like one of the terrorists who'd gunned down innocent men and women.

Grace found a cell phone in a side pouch and touched the power button. Nothing happened. The screen wasn't cracked, but the battery might be dead. On the outside of the bag, embroidered on a strip of camouflage, was the name O'Neill in bold green letters.

Grace would call the local police station and see what she could find out about the mysterious Mr. O'Neill. For now, all she could do was head home. She'd have to call and reschedule her interview when she wasn't bruised and dirty from having lain on the ground, crushed beneath a man who'd proven to be a hero.

Slipping one of the rucksack's straps over her shoulder, she headed for the metro station and caught the train out of the city to Alexandria where she shared an apartment with her roommate from college. Once on the train, she pulled her cell phone out of her pocket and searched through the recent calls for the one she'd taken to schedule the interview.

Once she found it, she dialed, lifted the device to her ear and covered her other ear.

"Halverson Enterprises, Margaret speaking," a woman's voice came on the line.

"This is Grace Lawrence. I was supposed to interview with Mrs. Halverson today."

"Oh, yes. I was just about to call and advise you Mrs. Halverson will not be available today. She has been regrettably detained."

"Oh," Grace said. "Okay."

"I've been asked to reschedule your interview for tomorrow morning at 8:30 a.m. Mrs. Halverson will see you then."

"Thank you. I look forward to meeting her."

"Wait," Margaret laughed. "You called me. Was there something I could help you with?"

"Oh, thank you but… I was just calling to confirm the interview," Grace said. Margaret didn't need to know Grace had called to say she couldn't make her scheduled appointment.

Grace ended the call and released a sigh. At least she hadn't blown her chances by being a no-show.

By the time Grace stepped off the train at her stop, the shock of the day had set in. Her knees shook as she walked the few blocks to her apartment complex, and she fumbled with her keys before she could open the front door.

Once inside, she set the rucksack on the floor, kicked off her heels, collapsed on the couch in the living room and dug her cell phone out of her purse.

A text message displayed across the screen.

Leaving work on time tonight. What's for supper?

The message was from early that morning. Grace had just noticed it. She snorted out a laugh, the sound catching on a sob. What a day. Her roommate, Riley Lansing, wouldn't believe what had happened to her. Grace would have to wait until Riley arrived at the apartment before she could tell her about it.

In the meantime, Grace needed to find out where O'Neill was and arrange to get his rucksack back to him.

She spent the next hour calling police stations, trying to locate the man, but with no luck. After hitting one brick wall after the other, she set her cell phone aside and wandered into the kitchen, looking for something to eat.

A glance at the clock on the stove made her frown.

Riley had said she'd be leaving work on time, which would have been over an hour ago.

Grace abandoned the refrigerator and retrieved her cell phone from the coffee table in the living room. She texted Riley.

Did you stop at the store?

She waited for Riley's response. When it didn't come, she tried again.

Hello? I thought you'd be home by now.

Grace shrugged and headed for the kitchen again. Perhaps Riley *had* stopped at a store with lousy reception, or her cell phone was buried at the bottom of her purse, or she'd turned off the sound. Riley wasn't one to say she'd be home on time and then take a lot longer, without calling.

A bad feeling washed over Grace. She tried to shrug it off as residual nerves from the earlier attack in DC. But the longer she waited for Riley, the more worried she became.

Since Grace had moved in, she and Riley were the other's support system. Grace's parents had been an older couple when Grace was born and had since passed away. Riley's folks were on a world cruise and not sched-uled to be back for another twenty days.

Grace called Riley's number and listened to it ring six times before it went to her voice mail. She called again and the voice mail picked up immediately.

She left a message. "Riley, call me. I'm worried about you."

By midnight she was past being worried and beginning to become frantic. She called the police and reported her roommate as missing.

"How long has she been missing?" the dis-patcher asked.

"At least five hours. She's never late. She texted me this morning, saying she'd leave work on time tonight. Leaving work on time means she would have left more than five and a half hours ago."

"Could she have stopped at a friend's house?" the dispatcher asked.

"Not without calling to tell me," Grace said.

"Where is her last known location?" the woman on the other end of the line asked.

"She was leaving work at Quest Aerospace Alliance." Grace gave the address and waited.

"We'll have a unit check it out. If you hear from her, please let us know to call off the search."

"Thank you."

The dispatcher ended the call.

The simple act of reporting her friend as missing did nothing to allay Grace's fears. She couldn't stay in the apartment, waiting. She had to go out and look for herself. If the police found her in the meantime, they would contact her on her cell phone. She'd have it with her.

Grace scribbled a note to Riley and left it on the counter. If Riley came home while Grace was out, she was to call her immediately.

Grace shrugged into her jacket, grabbed her purse, slipped the Taser Riley had gifted her at Christmas inside the front pocket and left the apartment, heading...

Hell, she didn't even know which way to go.

Squaring her shoulders, she walked through the dark streets to the train station, her gaze searching the shadows for potential threats. When she reached the metro stop, she climbed aboard the train headed toward Quest Aerospace Alliance. She'd start there and work her way backward, praying she'd find Riley at a bar or hanging out with a friend.

Deep down, Grace knew she wouldn't. She was Riley's friend and they didn't have anyone else they hung out with.

Grace tucked her hand into the pocket of her purse, curling her fingers around the Taser it concealed. Riley had an identical device. She'd been the one who'd often insisted that they needed some kind of protection in the big city.

Grace didn't feel any safer, but a Taser was better than nothing. She just had to be prepared to use it. Perhaps Riley hadn't been as prepared. When she found Riley, she'd be sure to ask. Because she *would* find Riley. *Alive.*

DECLAN SPENT TWO hours in a holding room, where he was repeatedly grilled about his part in the attack in downtown DC. Thankfully, he'd had his wallet on him, but the majority of his money was in his rucksack. If…no…*when* he was released, he only had a five-dollar bill to get something to eat, but no money to get around. He might as well stay the night in the jail. At least he'd get a free meal and a bed to sleep on, out of the cold, rain or whatever the weather was doing outside.

The police had allowed him to make one phone call. When he'd dialed his number, the phone service indicated his phone was not online at that time. Meaning the battery was dead and the woman he'd entrusted all of his worldly goods to had yet to find or charge it.

His one call wasted, he was escorted back to the holding room, where he was questioned all over again by yet another detective.

"What organization are you with?" the detective asked.

"I'm not with any organization," Declan responded.

"Witnesses reported you were armed with a submachine gun. One like the other attackers carried."

"I was in the right place at the wrong time. I watched those men kill the security detail surrounding a limousine, and then they kidnapped that woman. While others stood around gawking, I took it upon myself to do something."

"So, you just waltzed in with your submachine gun and jumped into the back of a van?" The man snorted. "Highly unlikely."

"I was unarmed. However, I was able to disarm one of the attackers and confiscate his weapon."

"Convenient." The detective's lips pressed into a thin line. "By all accounts, the attackers were highly trained. How is it you were able to relieve one of them of his weapon?"

Declan shrugged. "You obviously aren't buying anything I have to say. Why should I bother talking to you?" He looked past the detective. "I want to talk to a lawyer."

The detective glared. "You'll be talking soon enough."

Though his hackles rose on the back of Declan's neck, he stared back at the detective, wiping all emotion from his face. "I'll talk when I have a lawyer."

The detective smirked. "You got one?"

"I will as soon as you let me make a call."

"You had your chance to make a call."

Declan sat back in his chair and crossed his arms over his chest.

The detective leaned forward, his lip curling back in a snarl. "Look here, jerk, I have ten dead tourists, nineteen injured, and the

DC mayor and the President of the United States breathing down my neck for answers."

Declan clamped his lips tight. He was done talking.

The door opened behind the detective and an older man in uniform stuck his head in the door. "Solomon, a word with you."

The detective gave Declan a narrow-eyed glance. "We're not through here."

As far as Declan was concerned, they were.

Detective Solomon left the room. A moment later, a different officer entered. "Mr. O'Neill, please come with me."

Declan rose, fully expecting to be led to the rear of the building and stuck in a cell. His stomach rumbled. He was all for being incarcerated if it meant getting a meal out of it.

Instead, the man led him out of the holding area and back to the front of the building.

A group of men in dark suits stood in a cluster around a woman. She waved them aside and strode toward him, her head held high, her blood-stained clothes worn like a suit of armor.

She was the woman he'd saved from the kidnappers.

"Declan O'Neill?" she asked.

"Yes, ma'am. That's me."

"You have been cleared of any charges. These kind officers are releasing you." She raised her eyebrows and stared around at the policemen standing by, as if challenging them to say anything different.

"I don't understand," he said.

"What do you not understand about your being released?" she asked. "I told them that you saved my life and fought valiantly against my attackers, risking your own life to save mine." She frowned. "I'm appalled they took you into custody to begin with. Thankfully, I wasn't the only one who witnessed your heroism. Between my account and those of others who were nearby, you've been cleared of any wrongdoing."

"Thank you, ma'am."

"Please don't call me ma'am. Makes me sound like your grandmother." She sniffed. "As well I could be. But that's neither here nor there. My name is Charlotte, but my friends call me Charlie. I prefer Charlie. And if you don't have a ride, I would gladly take you anywhere you want to go. And the sooner, the better. It's almost midnight, and I've had a hell of a day."

"Thank you, Charlie." Declan squared his shoulders. "I don't need a ride," he lied, unwilling to admit he was homeless, possessionless and broke.

"Then we'll wait until your ride arrives." The woman looked around, found a chair and promptly sat.

"You don't have to wait," Declan said. Appalled that he would be caught out in his lie.

"I want to make sure the police don't decide to reacquire their prisoner." She glared at the nearest officer. "He's not one of the terrorists who attacked me," she reiterated.

The officer held up his hands in surrender. "I'm not saying he is, but we can't have a crowd in the building. We have work to do."

The older woman harrumphed and rose to her feet. "Fine, we'll wait outside for Mr. O'Neill's transportation to arrive." She nodded toward the four men in suits. "Come along."

Charlie led the way to the exit. Before she could open the door, Declan stepped in front of her. "Let me," he said.

Charlie smiled. "Such a gentleman."

"No, ma'am." He stepped through the door and closed it in her face. After scanning the area around them, he turned and opened the door for her to come out.

She stood with her arms crossed over her chest, a frown wrinkling her brow. She leveled her glare at the men in suits. "You should have gone out first and checked for potential attackers. Instead, you let this young man do it for you." She flicked her fingers. "You're all fired."

The men in suits frowned. One of them stepped forward. "But—"

Charlie held up her hand. "Uh, uh, uh," she said. "No excuses. You may go home. I won't be needing your services." She dug in her purse and pulled out a one-hundred-dollar bill and handed it to the man who appeared to be in charge. "To get you back to your own transportation."

The man took the bill and left with the other three to find a taxi back to wherever they'd parked their vehicles.

Charlie sighed. "Now what am I supposed to do?" She gave Declan a bright smile. "I don't suppose you would like to come to work for me, providing my protection?"

A job? Declan didn't want to appear too needy, but hell, he'd just been offered a job.

"What exactly would it entail?"

"Oh, I don't necessarily want you to be a bodyguard. However, I'd want you to be in charge of hiring a bodyguard for me, or four or five. I lost three good men today. And two more are in the hospital, fighting for their lives. I'm tired of terrorists getting away with murder, and the authorities are doing so very little about it.

"And after I'm situated with personal protection, I might want you to do a lot more."

"More what?"

"More making things right where they've gone completely wrong."

He held up his hands. "I'm not into being a vigilante."

"And I'm not into spending years on red tape and bureaucratic nonsense while good, honest people are taking the fall, literally. Like today. Not that I'm all that good or honest, but what happened shouldn't have."

"Why did it happen? What did they want with you?"

"I'm sure they were going to hold me for ransom or some such nonsense. I'm loaded. Everyone always wants to get their hands on my money. Hell, if they asked for it nicely, I'd probably give it to them." Charlie waved her hand. "You haven't answered my question. Do you want a job or not?"

He wanted one, even if it was with a slightly deranged older woman. But she had to know the truth about him. "Don't you want to see my résumé, do a background check, see if I have a criminal record?"

She ran her gaze from his head to his toes. "I've seen all I need to see."

He bristled at her perusal. "I'm not a gigolo."

She laughed out loud. "Now, that conjures way too many tempting thoughts." Her smile faded. "Not that you're hard to look at. But I loved my dearly departed husband completely, despite what the tabloids might have said. I don't anticipate any man filling his shoes anytime soon, if at all."

With the possibility of being hired as a sex toy cleared up, Declan still had one more obstacle. "I was dishonorably discharged from the US Marine Corps." There, he said it flat out. It still hurt to say the words. He'd put his entire life into his career as a Force Recon marine.

Charlie slipped her purse over her shoulder. "I know."

Declan stared at the woman, shocked. "You know?"

"You don't think I'd offer you a job if I didn't know what I was getting into, do you?" She looked at him with raised eyebrows.

"No, ma'am."

"Charlotte or Charlie. Not ma'am." She held out her hand. "You're coming to work for me?"

He hesitated only a moment longer before

taking her hand. "Yes, ma'—" he took her hand "—Charlie."

"How soon can you start?" she asked.

"As soon as you want me," he said. "Preferably sooner than later. I don't have a ride and the five dollars in my wallet is going toward a hamburger."

"Dear Lord, why didn't you say so?" She nodded toward the parking lot. "I'm hungry, too. I haven't had a decent hamburger since I hired a French chef. It's well past time to indulge." She held out her arm.

Declan gripped her elbow and glanced at the parking lot, where a long black limousine stood, blocking police cruisers into their parking spaces. He chuckled. "I'm surprised you don't have a handful of tickets on that boat."

"I left my driver in the driver's seat for just such an occasion." She waited for him to open the door before slipping inside. Charlie patted the seat beside her. "I'd feel better if you rode back here with me. Although, you might not want to. My other bodyguards—God rest their souls—didn't fare well earlier today." Her smile dipped into a frown. "Those bastards deserve to die for killing my men and all of those innocent bystanders."

Declan slid into the back seat, next to Charlie.

She captured his gaze with a shadowed gray one of her own. "Don't you see? Those are the kinds of wrongs I want to right. I have more money than I could ever spend. I want to do something to help others. If it means going around the law to see it's done right... so be it."

"I'm not in the habit of breaking the law, despite my lousy military record," he warned her.

"I'm not asking you to break the law. Maybe bend a few rules, but not exactly break the law." She reached for his hand. "Sometimes the authorities get in the way of justice or let people off who we know good and well are as guilty as sin. I've seen it happen more often than I'd care to admit. Someone like me, with more money than sense, buys his way out of jail or buys his son or daughter's way out of serving time. No one should get away with murder." Her hand clutched his tightly.

"Why are you so passionate about this?" he asked.

For a moment, she stared down at his hand. Then she released it and stared out the window. "My husband was murdered. The police got nowhere. No matter how much money I threw at private investigators, they couldn't tell me who pulled the trigger. I know how I felt, losing my husband, who should have been around to grow older with me. I don't want others to have to go through what I did."

"I'll work for you and do what I can," Declan said. "But I won't break the law."

"Unless you have to in order to save a life," Charlie said. "I had to pay a big bribe to get you out of hot water for using that submachine gun."

Declan hadn't considered the fact he might have been breaking the law when he took up the gun.

Charlie nodded with a smug smile. "That's right. Possessing that kind of weapon isn't legal in DC."

Declan cursed beneath his breath. "I didn't know. All I was worried about was saving you."

"I know that, and you know that." She sighed. "But the law is clear. If you're caught in possession of a submachine gun, you can be thrown in jail. Again, some rules are meant to be bent. You wouldn't have saved my life if you hadn't snagged that man's weapon and used it on his cohorts."

Declan had once again backed himself into a corner of his own doing. If not for Charlie's ability to sway the police force with a sizable contribution, he wouldn't be free. He'd be sitting on a hard cot in a cell. "How much do I owe you? All I can do is work it off."

Charlie touched his arm. "No, dear. I owe you my life. The least I could do was make sure you weren't blamed for something you didn't do." She pressed a button on the armrest and the window between the driver and the rear of the vehicle slid downward.

"Carl, could you stop at the next corner? I believe there's a hamburger establishment there."

"Excuse me?" Carl glanced back at them through the rearview mirror, his expression incredulous. "Hamburger?"

"You heard me. And not one word to Francois, my chef. He would be appalled to know I had eaten something as banal as a hamburger with extra onions and pickles."

Declan sat back against the seat, wondering

just who this woman was and why she'd decided to hire him on the spur of the moment.

He was grateful for the opportunity to work and earn an honest paycheck, but he wondered if there was more to Charlie than met the eye.

Time would tell. For now, Declan was grateful for the wealthy woman and the hamburgers they ordered at the drive-through window. Or rather, the hamburgers the driver ordered, paid for and received on their behalf.

Declan leaned across the seats to grab the bag of burgers and fries, the scent nearly crippling him, he was so hungry.

The next few minutes were spent in silence as Charlotte, Declan and the driver consumed the food, washing it down with iced tea.

When Charlie asked where Declan lived, he knew it was useless to lie. "I'm new in town," he said, avoiding an answer rather than attempting a lie.

"Oh, so you haven't had time to check into a hotel?"

"No, ma'am…er… Charlie. But I'll be fine."

"Getting a hotel at this late hour can be hit and miss." She talked to the driver by using the intercom. "Carl, take us home." Charlie patted Declan's arm. "You'll stay at my house until you can get a place of your own. I'll start you out with funds to set you up in an apartment as part of your pay."

Declan stiffened. "I can't accept your charity."

"Oh, I wouldn't call it charity." She sat back on the leather seat. "You will be earning your pay in my employ." She patted her belly. "And that was perhaps the best hamburger I've had in a very long time."

"Charlie, I can't do this. I've never in my life taken advantage of a woman's generosity."

She lifted her chin and stared down her nose at him. "Oh, believe me, I have plans for you. You'll earn every dime working for Halverson Enterprises."

With no other choices to fall back on, Declan squared his shoulders and faced his future.

Chapter Three

Grace stood outside of the Halverson Enterprises building near K Street at 8:20 a.m.,
feeling like she'd been hit by a truck, and
probably looking like it. She'd spent the majority of the night retracing what she would
have thought would be Riley's route on her
way home the evening before.

The guard at the gate to Riley's office complex had refused to let her in, insisting that
the building was closed for the night. She'd
have to return in the morning and talk with
the security supervisor. He didn't seem to understand that the morning might be too late.

The train held no clues as to Riley's where-abouts, and the path between the office complex and the train was clean of any traces of Grace's roommate.

The police had done a perfunctory investigation, running into the same issues as Grace and coming up as empty-handed as she had, and they hadn't contacted her in the past three hours.

She'd even tried calling Riley's supervisor. But all she had was his work number. The connection went straight to his voice mail.

Riley was missing, and Grace had an interview for a job she could care less about as long as her friend and roommate remained missing. Still, she could have stayed at her apartment and hoped Riley would stroll through the door, announcing she'd spent the night with a hot guy she met at a bar. But the waiting would have killed Grace.

Instead, she'd showered, blow-dried her hair and applied a minimal amount of makeup.

Dressed in a tailored skirt suit, she'd tucked her cell phone in her purse and left the ring-tone on high in case Riley actually called. Grace didn't care if she was in an interview or a meeting with the President of the United States—she'd answer the phone.

After taking a deep breath, she strode through the glass doors and stepped up to the reception desk.

The woman took her driver's license and handed her a visitor's pass. "Mrs. Halverson is expecting you."

Tears welled in Grace's eyes and she almost turned around and ran.

"It's okay," the woman at the reception desk whispered. "Mrs. Halverson is a really nice lady. You'll do fine."

Blinking to clear her vision, Grace nodded.

"Twelfth floor, straight out of the elevator. Her secretary will greet you."

"Thank you." Grace choked on her words and turned toward the elevator.

The receptionist held out a tissue. "You might want this." She gave her a warm smile. "Really, she's nice."

Grace nearly lost her composure there, but held it together long enough to make it into the elevator, where she waited until the door closed before she let the tears fall. But only a few. She was afraid she wouldn't be able to read the screen on her cell phone if she cried too much.

For the hundredth time, she checked for text messages from Riley.

Nothing.

The floor numbers flashed green on the display panel as the elevator car rose to the top of the office building.

Grace dabbed at her eyes, sure her mascara was running by now. What a great impression she'd make on Mrs. Halverson, a sobbing, hot mess of a woman in a wrinkled suit, with red-rimmed eyes and a runny nose.

Grace didn't care. Riley was still missing.

The elevator stopped.

As the doors opened, Grace jabbed at the buttons to go back down, but it was too late. Mrs. Halverson's secretary spotted her and smiled. "Miss Lawrence, I'm so glad you could make it after we stood you up yesterday. I'm Margaret Berkman." She rounded to the front of her desk and held out her hand.

Short of being completely rude, Grace was forced to step out of the elevator, cross to the secretary's desk and shake the woman's hand. "You didn't stand me up. I was caught up in the shooting yesterday. I didn't even make it to this building."

The woman's eyes widened. "Oh, dear. You will have so much to share with Mrs. Halverson. She was there, too." The secretary turned toward the door behind her. "Come with me."

"If she was there yesterday, perhaps now isn't a good time to conduct this interview." The timing was terrible for Grace. She felt as if she would break down at any moment.

"Mrs. Halverson was looking forward to meeting you. I'm sure she will be fine."

Mrs. Halverson might be fine, but Grace certainly wasn't.

She squared her shoulders, glanced at her cell-phone screen again and followed Margaret into a spacious office with a wide solid-mahogany desk. A gray-haired woman sat with her back to the door, staring out at the buildings making up the skyline of Washington, DC.

When Mrs. Halverson turned, she smiled and pushed to her feet. "Miss Lawrence, so very nice to meet you."

Grace gasped. The woman was the same one who'd been yanked out of the limousine the day before and hauled into the kidnapper's van. "You...you were the one."

Mrs. Halverson frowned. "Pardon me?"

Grace shook her head slowly. "You were the woman at the shooting yesterday. The one they tried to kidnap."

Mrs. Halverson clasped Grace's hand in hers and nodded, her lips pressing into a thin line. "Yes, that was me. But that was yesterday, and I prefer to push it out of my thoughts. Horrible event. Just horrible." She drew in a deep breath and let it out on a sigh. "You're here to interview for the position of personal assistant, am I right?"

Grace didn't move from where she stood, her mind spinning with the frightening memories of the day before. "Are you all right?" she asked.

"I'm fine," she said, a shadow crossing her face. "But I lost some good men in that disaster. Fine men with families."

"They didn't hurt you?" Grace asked.

Mrs. Halverson smiled. "Thankfully, a nice young man rescued me from the kidnappers before they could take me to parts unknown." She frowned and stared at Grace. "You were there?"

Grace nodded. "I was. I think the man who

rescued you saved me before he went after you."

Mrs. Halverson's lips twitched upward. "Sounds like what he would do. That young man doesn't think about his own safety. He's too busy saving everyone else. And the police had the nerve to arrest him."

So, that's what had happened to him after he'd left his backpack in Grace's care.

"But enough about me. Tell me about you," Mrs. Halverson said. She waved a hand toward several leather chairs arranged around a low coffee table.

Grace shook her head. "I... I can't do this."

"Do what? Have a conversation with me?" Mrs. Halverson took Grace's arm. "I tell you, I'm okay. I really need a personal assistant. Otherwise I'd reschedule."

"You don't understand." Grace pulled her arm free of Mrs. Halverson's grip. "Yesterday was bad on more levels than just the attack downtown." She shook her head, her heart pinching hard inside her chest. "My room-mate didn't come home last night. I've been worried sick and combing the streets, look-ing for her." The tears welled again and some spilled over, sliding down her cheek. "Mrs. Halverson, I'm afraid I can't do this inter-view."

Mrs. Halverson drew Grace into her arms and led her to a sofa. She settled her there and held her at arm's length. "Tell me what hap-pened. When did she go missing?"

Grace told her what she knew, where she'd gone and how she'd contacted the police. Tears slipped from her eyes and trailed down her cheeks.

The older woman shook her head. "I'm sorry about your friend. I'd be worried, too." She lifted Grace's chin and stared into her eyes. "But you've come to the right place. I think I might be able to help."

Grace laughed, her voice choking on a sob. "How can you help? The police couldn't do anything. I couldn't find her." She sucked in a shaky breath and let it out. "I don't know what else to do."

Mrs. Halverson patted her hand. "I know someone who might be of assistance. And this is just the kind of thing I hired him for."

"You do?" Using the tissue the receptionist had given her, Grace scrubbed the tears from her eyes. "Who?"

Mrs. Halverson stood. "You stay right there." She walked to the door, poked her head out and said, "Send in my new hire. I have a job for him."

Mrs. Halverson returned to the couch and drew Grace to her feet. "I'm sure he'll be able to help you. He's a trained warrior and quite good at it."

"A warrior?" Grace shook her head. "I need a tracking dog."

"I'm sure he can do that. He's pretty versatile." She smiled and looked past Grace. "Ah, there you are." Mrs. Halverson turned toward the door. "Declan, meet Grace Lawrence."

Grace turned and her jaw dropped. She knew this man.

Mrs. Halverson continued. "Grace, this is Declan—"

"O'Neill," Grace finished.

The older woman frowned. "You know each other?"

Declan nodded while Grace shook her head.

"I have your rucksack," Grace said. "I didn't know how to find you."

"I tried to call my cell phone, but the battery must have died." He held out his hand. "What were the chances we'd find each other here?"

Mrs. Halverson shrugged. "Since you two know each other, I'll leave you both to the task of finding Miss Lawrence's roommate. I have a lot to do." She drew in a deep breath and let it out slowly, a shadow passing over her face. "Arranging for the funerals of my bodyguards." She stared at Grace. "As for the job—are you still interested?"

Grace nodded. "I am, but I need to find my roommate before I can get my head on straight."

Mrs. Halverson shook her head. "You need to get your head on straight to *find* your roommate. Once you do, come back for that interview. I still need an assistant, but I can wait." She nodded to Declan O'Neill. "Now that you've located your rucksack and phone, you can contact your friends. I'm sure they'll make fine additions and can assist you in our new venture. Remind me, we need to come up with a name for your team."

"Yes, ma'am—" O'Neill caught himself and smiled. "Thank you, Charlie. I'll do my best to help Miss Lawrence."

"Now, if you'll clear out of my office," Mrs. Halverson said, "I have some calls to make. Keep me up to date on your discoveries."

"We will," O'Neill said. He hooked Grace's arm and led her out of the office.

Mrs. Halverson's secretary stood as they closed the door behind them. "How did the interview go?" Margaret asked with a smile.

"It didn't," Grace responded.

Margaret's smile fell. "I'm sorry to hear it. I'm sure she has her reasons, but I was hoping she'd find an assistant. She really needs one."

Grace gave her a gentle smile. "The interview has been postponed. I'll be back soon." She glanced up at the man Mrs. Halverson had called Declan O'Neill. "In the meantime, Mr. O'Neill and I have work to do."

She didn't know this man from Adam, but having witnessed his military prowess under the stress of being fired upon, she had no doubt he'd be of some assistance. And knowing she had someone to help her find Riley made her more optimistic than she'd been since her roommate had gone missing.

The secondary fact that O'Neill was muscular, ruggedly handsome and skilled with his hands made Grace quiver inside. Not that he'd use those hands on her. Preferably, he'd use them to take down whoever had snatched Riley and make him pay for any harm that might have come to her friend.

"Where do you want to start?" he asked.

"Where she works," Grace said. "They wouldn't let me in last night."

"We can do a preliminary call to her supervisor and ask what time she actually walked out of the building," O'Neill said.

Grace nodded. "And if that doesn't help, we can ask the people at the front desk when she came through," Grace suggested.

"After that?" he asked.

"I don't know what else to do other than canvass the train station at the time she would have been there. I have a recent photograph of her on my cell phone. We can ask people getting on and off the train if they saw her last night."

O'Neill led the way to the elevator, punched the down button and then turned to face her. "We can also check with the train service to see if they have video cameras and historical data we can go through."

"Good thinking," Grace said.

The elevator door slid open and Grace stepped inside.

Her newly assigned private investigator stepped in beside her.

O'Neill's broad shoulders made the elevator feel so much smaller and seemed to suck the air right out of her lungs.

She focused on what was important, her missing roommate. But that didn't keep the heat from rising beneath the starched collar of her shirt.

Sure, a man like O'Neill could turn any woman's head. But Grace had been divorced for three years, and her husband had been hot. Maybe not muscular, he-man hot like O'Neill, but he'd turned his share of heads and ruffled a few female skirts before he'd asked Grace to marry him.

She'd been flattered and fancied herself in love with him. And then he'd changed. Perhaps *changed* wasn't exactly right. His true colors came through. Mitchell had been full of himself and wrapped up in his business as a high-powered financial planner. He'd wanted everything his way, never considering Grace's needs and desires. She'd gone along with his plans at first, but no more. She wouldn't be cowed by any man ever again.

Grace could admire the beauty of nature in a handsome man, but she didn't have to pluck the flower or sip the nectar. She performed an internal eye-roll. As she'd told Mrs. Halverson, she had to get her head on straight. What was important was finding Riley.

The elevator door opened and Grace practically jumped out. As she did, her cell phone rang. Her heart racing, she dug in her purse, her hands shaking so much that she couldn't get them to work.

"Good grief," Declan said. "Give it to me." He took the purse, dug his hand in, found the phone and hit the answer key. Then he handed it to Grace.

She shot a glance at the screen but didn't recognize the number. Grace pressed the phone to her ear, praying whoever it was would have news of her friend. "Hello?"

"Grace Lawrence?"

"That's me."

"This is Sergeant Kronkski with the DC Metropolitan Police Department."

Grace's heart stopped beating. "Go on," she whispered, her breath lodging like a knot in her throat.

"We just wanted to keep you up to date on your missing person's report."

"Have you found Riley?" she asked, her hand gripping the cell phone tightly.

"No, ma'am. We haven't. You said the last

place you had contact with her was from her place of employment yesterday?"

"That's right. I told the officer on duty that last night."

"We sent a unit by her office complex this morning. They have no record of her being at work yesterday. She didn't clock in."

Grace frowned, her gaze going to Declan.

He took the phone and punched the speaker key before handing it back to her.

"What do you mean, she never clocked in? She texted me from work yesterday morning. Riley never missed a day of work, even when she was sick."

"That's what we were told. Her supervisor confirmed she never arrived at the office yesterday."

"That can't be right," Grace said, shaking her head, though the sergeant wouldn't see the effect. "She went to work like always and texted me that she would be leaving on time."

"Some people live secret lives," the sergeant

said. "Perhaps she has another job you don't know about?"

"No way. Riley doesn't keep secrets from me. We're friends from our first year in college."

"I can only tell you what we learned," the sergeant said. "Is there anywhere else she might have gone? To see family? A friend? A boyfriend?"

Grace's lips pressed together. "She said she was coming home. She has no other family in the country but me, her roommate. Her parents are on a world cruise, out of touch most of the time. She's not married and, as far as I know, she doesn't have a boyfriend."

"Okay, I get it," the sergeant said. "But these are the questions I have to ask. More often than not, missing people haven't been abducted. They've ducked out of sight, either running from the law or needing some space."

"I know my roommate," Grace said. "She

wouldn't have told me she was coming home and then not shown up without calling to say why. She's conscientious and considerate like that. If she'd been detained or changed her mind, she would have called or texted me to let me know she was all right."

"I'm sorry we don't have more news, but I wanted to let you know where we stood. We have her picture out to all the street units now. If they see her, you'll be notified."

Grace let go of the breath she'd been holding. Getting mad at the cops wasn't conducive to securing their help in finding Riley. Grace sucked it up and thanked the sergeant. "I appreciate the update and look forward to hearing from you soon." Really soon. Riley's life could depend on it.

Chapter Four

Declan stood in front of Grace throughout the cell-phone conversation. When she hung up, he took the phone from her and captured her hand in his. He was surprised at how much he liked the feel of her long, slender fingers. "We'll find her."

She stared down at where their hands interlocked. "I don't know how you can say that with such assurance when even the police can't find her." Her chin lifted and she stared into his eyes. "Riley's all I have. She's more than a friend. She's like family."

"All the more reason for us to get on this

right away." He pulled her hand through the crook of his elbow and walked with her toward the exit. "Do you have a vehicle, or are we going to take the train?"

"I have an SUV, but where are we going?" Grace's hand curled around Declan's elbow and she skipped to keep up with his pace.

"To Riley's workplace." Declan had to get a feel for the street and the path to the train station to better understand how Riley could have disappeared.

"They're a secure facility," Grace said. "They won't just let us walk in without an appointment."

"Do you know Riley's supervisor?" He stopped at the curb and looked around.

"I know his name." Grace pointed toward the parking lot. "I'm parked over there. The charcoal SUV."

He held out his hand. "Mind if I drive?"

She frowned. "And if I do?"

Declan shrugged. "It might be hard for

you to drive and call Riley's supervisor at the same time."

"I'm calling her supervisor?" Grace dug in her purse for her keys.

"Yes, you are. On the way to her workplace, call him and see if he will let us in to talk to him about Riley."

Grace handed him the keys. "I tried calling him earlier, but he was out of the office or hadn't come to work yet. The call went straight to his voice mail."

"Try again." He stepped off the curb and strode toward the parking lot.

Grace steered him toward her vehicle.

Before they reached it, Declan clicked the remote to pop the locks open. He held the passenger door for Grace and waited while she settled in the seat. Then he closed the door and rounded the front of the SUV. It was smaller than the vehicle he'd sold before his last deployment, but it was roomy enough to accommodate his six-foot-three frame without bumping his head.

He slid into the driver's seat, adjusted it for his height and started the engine. Before he shifted into gear, he turned to Grace. "GPS directions?"

She tapped the screen on her cell phone.

With the cell-phone voice calling out the route, Declan backed out of the parking space and shifted into Drive.

Grace called Riley's supervisor and waited while the line rang. She shifted the call from her phone to the car speaker so that Declan could hear the conversation.

"Quest Aerospace Alliance. Alan Moretti speaking."

"Mr. Moretti? This is Grace Lawrence, Riley's roommate."

Declan turned onto the road leading to one of the main arteries through town.

A long pause greeted Grace's announcement.

"Miss Lawrence, I'll tell you what I told

the police. Miss Lansing never showed up for work yesterday. I don't know where she is."

Declan touched Grace's arm and whispered, "Appointment."

"I have nothing more to add to my statement," Moretti said. "I'm sorry your friend is missing, but I had nothing to do with it."

"I understand, Mr. Moretti. But could you spare a few minutes to meet me in person? I have a few questions I'd like to ask for myself."

"I'm sorry, but no," he said. "I repeat, I have nothing to add." A click ended the call.

Grace stared down at the phone. "Now what?"

"We go to Quest Aerospace Alliance and figure this out." Declan frowned. He hadn't liked Mr. Moretti's answers. "You say Riley texted you from work yesterday?"

"That's right," Grace said. She touched the screen on her cell phone and brought up her text messages. "She specifically said she was leaving work on time that night."

Declan glanced at the cell-phone display screen as he paused at a red traffic light. Grace had repeated Riley's message verbatim.

"Why would she say she was leaving work on time if she was somewhere else?" Grace asked.

"Would she ever have played hooky from work?" Declan asked.

"No. She's a very conscientious person. She wouldn't lie, and she's a rule follower."

"Was she involved in a relationship with someone?" Declan asked.

Grace shook her head. "No. She said she didn't have time. She lived her job."

"How long has she been your roommate?"

"This time or in college?" she asked as they crossed the Potomac and drove into Arlington, Virginia.

"Anytime. Tell me everything. You never

know what little bit of information is important. What is your relationship with Riley? What does she do at Quest Aerospace?"

Grace drew in a deep breath. "Riley and I were roommates in college. We were assigned the same dorm room as freshmen and stayed friends throughout. While I went into political science, she studied engineering." Grace smiled. "She was much better at math than I was." She glanced his way. "Then we went in different directions after college. I worked on Capitol Hill for the previous administration, met a guy and got married. My career went on hold for him. He wanted a trophy wife, someone to stay home, cook, clean and entertain for him." She shook her head. "Archaic, right?"

Declan's chest tightened and he shot a glance at Grace's bare ring finger. "You're not wearing a ring now."

Grace snorted softly. "Yeah, I wasn't very good at being a second-class citizen, and my brain was getting mushy from too many sit-coms on television."

Declan knew there was little chance Grace's marriage had anything to do with Riley's dis-appearance, but he couldn't help asking, "So, you left your husband?"

Grace nodded. "I consider my marriage as one of my greatest failures and learning experiences. Failure in my ability to recog-nize a person's true character, and learning how to rebuild my life." She sucked in a deep breath and let it out slowly. "I'd kept up with Riley all through the past few years, calling every three or four months to see how she was doing in her career. I envied her ability to focus and go for what she wanted. Since my parents are gone, she was the first per-son I called when my divorce was final. She insisted I move in with her until I get on my feet. I put it off for a couple of years and fi-nally gave in a few months ago."

"Is that why you were interviewing for the

job with Mrs. Halverson? Are you new in the area?"

With a smile, Grace shook her head. "No, I took other odd jobs, working for a temp agency, but I wanted something more full-time and as permanent as can be expected in this day and age."

Declan twisted his lips. "Something along the lines of your political science major?"

"I really don't know what I want. To feel needed, perhaps. As a personal assistant to a high-powered woman, I was sure to be needed." She cringed. "Sounds pathetic, but there you have it."

"And Riley? Was she ever married?"

"No." Grace stared straight ahead. "At least she got that right. She focused on her career."

"Did she date? Have a boyfriend?"

"She did see a guy for a while after she graduated college, but he was heading for the military. She wasn't ready to follow him to parts unknown and give up her opportunity to gain experience in her own field of aerospace engineering."

"Any harsh feelings between them at their parting?" Declan asked.

"From what Riley told me back then, they left on mutual agreement and good terms."

"No brokenhearted, lovesick ex who could have come back to claim what he thought was his?"

"No." Grace twisted her hands in her lap. "That's what has me worried. As far as I know, she didn't have an enemy in this world."

Declan glanced toward her briefly. Grace seemed to be a person who would trust a friend completely. "Are you sure you know all there is to know about your friend Riley?"

"She worked. Sometimes to excess, and that left her with little time for a life outside of the office. Some nights she'd go for a beer at a local pub. I went with her on occasion. She always wanted to stay longer than I did. But she always came home."

"A lone woman in this city? Isn't that dangerous?" Declan asked.

"Lots of women get around this city all by themselves." Grace drew in a deep breath and let it out. "She knows how to defend herself. She showed me some of her moves. Riley is quite capable of fighting off an attacker."

"If she was, she might not be missing."

Grace's brow dipped low. "Unless it was someone she knew."

"Since she worked so much, most of the people she knew—"

"—were the people she worked with." Grace stared across the console at Declan. "We need to get inside Quest and ask some questions."

In Crystal City, Declan pulled into a parking lot across from the high-rise building that was Quest Aerospace Alliance and parked in a slot facing the building.

"Why did you stop here? Shouldn't we try to get inside?" Grace asked.

"We need to study the building and look

for weaknesses. Since we can't get in without an appointment, we need to find another way to gain access. When I was with the Marine Force Recon teams, we did a lot of reconnaissance missions prior to conducting an operation. It gave us the intel we needed to make the effort go smoothly."

"Force Recon? What's that?"

"We're part of the Marine Special Operations Command."

"Are you like the army's Special Forces and the Navy SEALs?"

"Yes. Only Force Reconnaissance teams focus on marine expeditionary and amphibious operations."

"Reconnaissance, huh?"

"And direct-action operations, usually based on the reconnaissance and intel gathered."

Grace's eyes narrowed. "I thought you military types threw in hand grenades and lobbed mortars prior to going in. You know, the whole shock-and-awe thing."

Declan's lips twitched upward. "We have a little more finesse most of the time. But we do have occasions when we use the noise and big bangs."

Grace nodded, mockingly. "Teach me, oh wise one. Frankly, I don't care if you were a member of the Navy SEALs, Army Rangers or the local VFW, as long as we find Riley."

His lips twitched again. "The fact Quest is claiming she never showed up for work makes me suspicious. I think it merits getting inside and snooping around."

"If they're lying about Riley never showing up—" Grace tapped a finger to her chin "—it makes me wonder what they're trying to hide. Riley wouldn't have lied to me about leaving the office if she hadn't been there at all."

"How long have you been roommates this time with Riley?" Declan asked.

"Four months."

"And how long had you been living apart?"

Grace tipped her head to the side and used her fingers to count silently. "Seven years."

Declan glanced her way. "A lot could change in seven years."

"I know, but Riley is still the same Riley. She's smart."

"How long has she been with Quest?"

"Two years. She took a demotion to go to work for Quest. She said she wanted to get back into more project design and Quest was doing some innovative things."

"Like?"

"I'm not quite sure. Riley couldn't talk about it. She said it was all hush-hush to keep others from stealing their ideas and data."

"Which would be a good reason to restrict entry into the facility," Declan said. "How did Riley get in?"

"She had a badge she used to get in and out of the building. I had to take it to her once when she forgot it."

Grace rested her fingers on the door handle. "Now that we're here, what's next?"

Declan reached across and rested his hand on hers. "We watch the people coming and going from the building."

Grace's eyebrows lowered. "How is that going to help us find Riley?"

"Be patient," he said. "You'll see. It'll be lunchtime soon." He watched the gate. Several delivery trucks arrived and were allowed to enter the gate after the guard checked his computer tablet and shined a light into the rear of the truck. If he could get into the back of one of the delivery vehicles, he might make it past the guard and onto the compound.

People parked in the lot beside the building, and they entered and exited the gate on foot. As the hour approached noon, a rush of people left the building and walked a couple blocks to a row of food trucks and cafés.

"How are you at flirting?" Declan asked as he pushed the door open on the SUV.

"Flirting?" Grace stared at him as if he'd lost his mind.

"You know, batting your eyes and saying things you know will make a guy want to talk to you." He winked. The woman was beautiful. She'd have no trouble getting attention. "Really all you have to do is smile and you'll have a guy's complete attention."

Her cheeks blossomed with color.

Declan couldn't help but think Grace's husband must have been a jerk. This woman was beautiful and cared about the people she loved. All she needed was a little attention and she seemed to come alive.

Declan rounded the vehicle and held the door for Grace. She dropped to the ground and placed a hand on his arm to steady herself. "Who do I need to flirt with, and what am I trying to gain by it?"

"We can gain information, maybe even borrow an employee badge."

"Borrow?" She shook her head. "I told you I didn't want to do anything illegal."

"I said borrow. We'll give it back, or leave it at the front desk."

Grace chewed on her bottom lip, the movement distracting Declan more than he cared to admit. "I've never deceived anyone in order to break into a place."

"Neither have I." He took her hand and turned her to face him. "Do you want to get inside Quest and find out the truth about your friend Riley?"

Grace's eyes narrowed. "I do." She squared her shoulders and met his gaze. "Whatever it takes…short of committing a major crime, of course."

His lips twitched. "A minor crime is okay then?"

"We'll borrow the badge, with the full intention of returning it once we're done with it." She squeezed his hand and let go. "We'd better hurry before lunch is over."

As they neared the first café, Declan studied the people sitting at different bistro tables on the sidewalk. "It might be better to split up. Are you okay working on your own? I'll be nearby if you need me."

Grace nodded, her gaze on the people settling in to enjoy their meals. "I'll be okay."

Declan slowed to look at a menu affixed to a stand out front of one of the cafés. He wasn't hungry, but he pretended to peruse the menu while Grace searched for a spot in the open seating area outside the packed restaurant. The crowd worked in her favor. She was able to find a place at a table with a man who sat alone. A man who had a Quest badge clipped to his pocket.

Fighting the urge to smile, Declan weaved through the tables and stopped at the one behind Grace. Two middle-aged women occupied the table with a couple of spare seats. "Do you mind if I share your table?" he asked.

The two women smiled up at him.

One with auburn hair said, "We'd love the company."

The other with faded blond hair nodded. "What woman wouldn't want a handsome guy to share her table?"

"Thank you." Declan held out his hand. "I'm Dan."

The auburn-haired woman held out her hand. "Rachel and this is Joanne."

"Nice to meet you." He tipped his head toward the high-rise building. "Do you two ladies work at Quest?"

"We do. How about you?" Rachel stared across the table at Declan. "Do you work at Quest?"

"No, but I've thought about applying." He looked at the menu. "I hear it's a good place to work."

"It's work." Rachel grimaced. "But some days I find myself counting the days to retirement."

He glanced up. "Is it that hard?"

Rachel shrugged. "Not so much hard."

"It's just some managers are better than others," Joanne said.

"You get that just about anywhere you work," Declan commented.

Rachel sighed. "I know. I've outlasted three managers over the fifteen years I've worked at Quest. Some were good. One was bad. I've learned to keep my head down and my mouth shut, and eventually the bad manager will move on."

"Some take longer to move on than others," Joanne muttered and stuffed a bite of her salad into her mouth.

Rachel reached out to pat her friend's hand. "Just do like I said and keep a low profile. You'll be there fifteen years before you realize they've passed."

Joanne snorted. "Or disappear into oblivion."

Declan's attention zeroed in on Joanne's last comment. "Disappear?"

"Yeah, disappear." Joanne leaned forward. "I heard one of the engineers in special projects didn't show up for work this morning. People are speculating that she was let go." Joanne shook her head. "They don't—" she made quote marks with her fingers "—let go of people out of the special projects area. They know too much."

Declan leaned forward, his brows dipping, giving Joanne his full attention. "What do you mean? They don't let people leave their jobs?"

The dingy blonde's eyes narrowed and her voice dropped to just above a whisper. "It's like a mob. Once you're in the secret circle, you can never get out."

"Joanne, you don't know that." Declan raised his eyebrows, feigning shock. "That woman could have been canned for sharing those deep, dark secrets to someone outside the company. If the project died, they could have laid her off."

Joanne stared into Declan's gaze. "Whatever. She hasn't come back to work and the police have been asking about her. Everyone's talking about it."

Rachel touched Joanne's arm. "Shh. You're going to scare Dan."

He laughed. "Don't worry about me. It takes a lot to scare me. Besides, it's a great story."

Rachel's brow furrowed. "Are you a reporter?"

Declan held up a hand. "Good Lord, no." He spied a delivery truck that was parked along the street. A man in a dark uniform stepped out. "I'm a delivery-truck driver," he said. And if he wasn't mistaken, that delivery truck could be heading in the direction of the Quest building. He leaned forward and smiled at the women. "I just remembered something I forgot to deliver." He stood. "Please excuse me. I hope I didn't disrupt your meal too much."

"Oh, please." Rachel's lips twisted into a wry grin. "Having you at our table was a delight. Maybe you can come by at lunch every day."

"Thank you for sharing your table." Declan leaned forward and held out his hand to Rachel. As he did, he swept his other hand over her employee badge lying on top of her wallet. He did this, blocking Joanne's view of what he was doing. Then he closed this hand completely around the badge and shook Joanne's hand. "You two ladies made my day. It would be an honor to have lunch with you again." He winked and walked by Grace's table, pretending to accidentally bump into her. When he did, he dropped the badge into her open purse and walked away.

Once he was away from the café, he ducked between two buildings and circled around to emerge in the parking lot, where he'd seen the delivery van. The driver was stepping out of the van, carrying a large package.

When he entered a building, Declan slipped into the side door of the delivery van. A quick scan of the packages on the metal shelves indicated that many of them were destined for Quest. The back of the van contained larger packages that appeared to have been picked up along the man's delivery route.

Declan dropped low behind several larger boxes and stacked one of them even higher to keep the driver from spotting him.

Next to him, hanging from a metal shelf, were a couple of uniforms like the one the driver wore. On the lapel was a name tag with Rodney written in bold black letters.

The delivery van dipped slightly as the driver stepped aboard, engaged the engine and took off down the street.

While the vehicle was in motion, Declan texted Grace.

Found a ride in the back of a delivery van headed for Quest. Dropped ID badge in your purse. Get to Quest before the ladies I sat with leave the café. I'll find you inside.

Chapter Five

Grace had no trouble getting the man at the café table to talk to her. Hell, she couldn't get Jordan to shut up. When the text came through from Declan, she'd been hard-pressed to read it without appearing rude.

His message set her heart racing.

Declan had swiped a badge from one of the women he'd been sitting with and placed it in her purse?

Her breath caught in her throat and her pulse pounded so hard against her eardrums, she could barely hear the man talking to her across the table. "I'm sorry," she interrupted him. "I'm not feeling very well. Please, excuse me for a moment."

Jordan leaned forward, his brow furrowing. "Do you need me to go with you?"

"No, really. I don't think you'd want to go to the ladies' bathroom." She gave him a weak smile and patted her flat belly. "Stomach issues."

The waitress chose that moment to arrive with their food and set it on the table.

Grace pushed to her feet. "I need to go."

"What about your meal?" Jordan asked.

She dug in her purse for her wallet, feeling the hard plastic of the employee badge against her fingers. After tossing a bill on the table, she gave her tablemate another smile. "Thank you for the company and sharing your table. I'm sorry, but I think I'd better leave now."

As she passed the two women Declan had been with, one of them was looking at the table, a frown denting her forehead. "I know I brought it with me." She opened her wallet and looked inside, shaking her head. "It's not here."

A wave of guilt washed over Grace, making her stomach roil. She wasn't cut out to be a spy or secret agent. She could barely function with the guilt of knowing she possessed someone else's property. Especially when that someone was clearly disturbed by the loss. She almost went back to her and handed over the badge.

But she didn't. She was doing this to find Riley. The woman would get her badge back eventually; it was just a piece of plastic. Riley's life was more important.

With that in mind, she entered the café, weaved her way through the tables to the rear, where the bathrooms were and the back door.

Once outside, she walked down the alley, passing several buildings before emerging on the sidewalk leading to Quest. She fell in step behind a group of women walking the same direction. All of them had Quest employee badges clipped to their clothes or on lanyards around their necks. When they reached the gate, they swiped their cards at a reader before a turnstile. When the light on the reader turned green, they entered the campus.

Her hand shaking, Grace swiped her stolen badge and held her breath. The light turned green. She pushed against the turnstile, but it didn't move. Her pulse pounded and she thought she might pass out.

"Push a little harder. It can be a little stubborn at times," a woman said from behind her.

Grace pushed harder. The turnstile moved, allowing her to enter. Once through, Grace drew in a deep breath, bringing a rush of air into her oxygen-starved lungs. She'd made it.

The woman who'd been behind her smiled and passed her. "See? Just needs a little more oomph." She winked as she walked by.

Grace followed without catching up and blended in with others returning from lunch.

Once inside the building, she headed for the elevators like everyone else. Riley had said she worked on the eighteenth floor. Before she reached the elevator, a man in a delivery uniform stepped out of a hallway and approached her from the side.

"Excuse me, miss." He carried a large box that covered half of his face. "Could you hold the elevator for me?"

Grace entered the elevator, scooted to the side and pressed the button to hold the door open.

The delivery guy stepped in next to her, a little closer than she would have liked, but because of the crowd returning from lunch, she couldn't move over.

She pressed the button for the eighteenth floor. "What floor are you going to?" she asked.

"It's already lit up," he said, sounding vaguely familiar.

Afraid someone would say something about

not recognizing her, Grace kept her head down and waited as they stopped on what seemed like every floor in between the ground and the eighteenth.

At the sixteenth floor, everyone but the delivery guy had exited.

When the doors closed, Grace noticed the only button lit was for the eighteenth floor.

"I thought we would never be alone," the delivery man said, his voice so familiar, Grace shot a glance to his face.

"Declan."

He shook his head and tipped it toward a corner of the elevator car and whispered, "Security camera."

Her heart pounding, Grace had to focus on not looking toward the corners of the car. "Do you have a plan?" she whispered.

He chuckled and said equally softly, "I was hoping you did." Then he added, "Actually, my plan is simple. Gather info. Let's find her office. Ask some questions. Make observations."

Great. They were inside a building they had no business being in, headed for the floor Riley had worked on. They had no guarantee they'd get any farther on the employee badge Declan had swiped. Riley had been working in Special Projects and she'd been adamant about the level of secrecy for the project. To the point she didn't share any details with her closest friend, Grace.

The elevator tone sounded and the door slid open.

Fear gripped Grace, freezing her feet to the floor.

"We've got this. What's the worst they can do?" Declan whispered. "Kick us out?"

"Throw us in jail? Shoot us? Make us disappear like Riley?" Grace listed in a voice so low, she doubted Declan heard her.

His soft chuckle assured her he had heard and wasn't too worried.

Having him there bolstered her confidence enough so that she was able to move, placing her foot outside the elevator door, onto the smooth marble tile of the eighteenth floor.

The stark white walls and the white marble made her feel as if she were walking into a futuristic science-fiction movie. At any moment she expected an alien to appear in front of her and lead her to a special room where humans were dissected or probed.

A hysterical giggle rose up her throat. Grace swallowed hard to keep from letting it escape.

"Which way?" Declan asked.

"This is as much as I ever got from Riley. Eighteenth floor. That's it." Grace turned right. "She worked in Special Projects."

Declan pointed to a sign on the wall to the right. "This must be the place." The sign read SPECIAL PROJECTS.

At that moment, a man stepped through the door.

Grace caught a glance at his name tag.

Moretti.

She had to catch herself to keep from grabbing the man and shaking the truth out of him.

"Sir, could you hold the door? I have a delivery for Special Projects."

The man seemed distracted and in a hurry. He paused for a moment and backed into the room to hold the door.

"Thanks. I'll hold it for him," Grace offered.

"Good. I have work to do," Moretti said and then quickly left them in the open doorway.

Grace breathed a sigh as she walked past the ID-card scanner beside the door. Had she tried to use her stolen card, it might have set off alarms.

As it was, Moretti had probably just broken a rule by allowing them to enter without scanning a badge. He'd practically sprinted down the hallway to the elevator.

Grace let the door close between them in

case he decided he'd made a mistake and came back to demand identification.

The room they'd stepped into was a huge bank of cubicles with five-foot-high walls.

Declan leaned toward her ear. "Was that Moretti, your roommate's supervisor?"

She nodded.

His eyes narrowed. "Let's start in his office."

"Would be good to know where that is." Grace glanced around.

"Follow an outside wall," Declan said. "He's bound to have a door."

Grace turned right and walked along the outskirts of the cube farm, careful not to make eye contact with anyone in the aisles between the cubicles. She passed an office with a woman's name on a placard beside the door. The door was open, but no one was at the desk inside.

The next office had a sign indicating it was the duplication room. Inside were a couple of copiers, plus a large printer like those used to generate engineering or architectural drawings. It, too, was empty.

The next door was to a break room. The smell of coffee wafted out. A woman stood at a coffee maker, pouring a mug full of the dark brew.

At the corner of the large room was a larger office with a placard on the side of the door that read Director of Special Projects Alan Moretti.

The door was closed.

Grace reached out and twisted the handle, fully expecting it to be locked. It pushed open as if Moretti had left in such a hurry, he hadn't pulled it completely closed.

A quick glance around assured her there weren't any people close enough to notice her and Declan slipping into the office. And if they did, Grace would tell them that they were delivering a package for Mr. Moretti.

She entered, held the door for Declan and closed it as soon as he stepped through.

Once inside, Declan set the box on the floor and crossed to the desk.

"What exactly are we looking for?" Grace asked.

"Anything that might give us a clue as to what happened to Riley. A file, computer records, something belonging to Riley herself. Just look."

Grace twisted the lock on the door in case someone happened to hear them rummaging around inside the office.

Moretti had a fairly large office, with bookshelves on one side, a massive desk in the middle and a mini-bar with decanters filled with amber liquid. Huge windows stretched from floor to ceiling, with a view across the river of downtown Washington, DC, and some of the government buildings.

Declan sat behind the desk and tapped the keyboard.

Grace crossed to a door on the left. It led to a small closet. Inside was an umbrella and a freshly laundered suit and starched shirt still wrapped in the thin plastic from the dry cleaner's. An extra pair of patent-leather dress shoes rested on the floor of the closet. On the shelf above was a flashlight and a hard hat. Nothing that would indicate Riley's whereabouts.

Grace backed out of the closet and attempted to open a dark mahogany file cabinet, but it wouldn't budge. "Know how to pick a lock?" she asked.

"Know how to hack a computer?" Declan responded.

"As much as I know about picking a lock."

"Switch for a minute. Maybe you'll have more luck." He rose and passed her, touching her hand as he went. "It'll be okay. We'll find her."

"I hope you're right. The longer she's missing, the harder it will be."

"True. But we have to keep positive. For Riley." He pulled up his uniform pant leg and slipped a knife out of a scabbard strapped to his calf. He glided the knife between the lock and the drawer of the cabinet and popped the cabinet open.

"Show off." Grace shook her head, wishing she could slip a knife into the computer and pop the screen up.

She sat at Moretti's desk and wiggled the mouse. Most people couldn't remember the myriad of passwords required to function in the modern-day technical environment. Moretti couldn't be any different. He had to have a place he kept his passwords to include the one that got him onto the system.

Grace opened the top drawer on Moretti's desk. Nothing but pens, paper clips and business cards. She checked the drawers on either side and found a golf ball, a tee and golf gloves. In the drawer on the other side, she found a stack of magazines about airplanes, the space program and country living.

The man had a strange mix of reading material, but no bits of paper with computer passwords written on them. She ducked her head and checked the bottom of the desk. As she came up, she noticed something yellow beneath the keyboard.

When she lifted the keyboard, nothing was there. Turning the keyboard over, she found a yellow sticky note with the word *trinity* written followed by what appeared to be a date. Maybe a birthdate? She studied the name and the date.

"I can't see anything of interest in these files. It's mostly evaluation and training records of employees."

"Is Riley in there?"

"Yes, but all her folder has are some outstanding annual evaluations."

Grace set the yellow sticky note next to the computer keyboard and brought the screen to life by wiggling the mouse. The log-on popped up. She keyed in *trinity* and the date and waited.

Username or password failed

Grace tried again without the dashes in the date.

She waited for the computer to churn.

Seconds later, the same failure notice popped up.

Afraid to push the limit and lock out the log-on, she abandoned the computer and rose from the desk. On a cabinet behind her was a printer and supplies. The printer had a single sheet of paper lying in the output tray.

She lifted the sheet, turned it over and read.

Declan walked up behind Grace and looked over her shoulder. "What is it?"

A ripple of awareness washed over her. When Declan stood so near, Grace couldn't think straight. "Looks like the location of something," she said. "Let me plug it into my phone and see where it is."

Declan read off the number and street, while Grace keyed it into the map application on her cell phone.

"It's the Blue Gill Bar & Grill, about thirty minutes from here."

Voices sounded outside the door.

The metallic rasp of a key being pushed into the door lock alerted Grace and Declan.

"The closet." Declan grabbed Grace's hand and bolted for the only other door in the office. They had just ducked into the closet when the office door burst open.

Grace eased the closet door closed, leaving just enough of a crack to allow her to peer into the room.

Moretti hurried in, walking past the large box Declan had left in the middle of the room.

Grace held her breath, waiting for the man to say something about the box. If he'd expected the door to be locked, surely he would wonder how the box made it into the room.

But he didn't stop. Again, he appeared to be preoccupied. He walked across to the printer, snatched the paper with the address out of the tray and folded it to fit in his pocket.

He stopped at his desk and stared down at the screen, a frown furrowing his brow. He tapped the keyboard and shook his head. "Who am I kidding? I don't have time to go through my email." He turned toward the closet.

Grace shrank back against Declan, pressing into him, trying to fade into the farthest corner of the tiny space.

Declan's arm circled her waist, the solid muscles like a band of steel around her, making her feel a little safer.

A cell phone rang in the office. Moretti answered, "Yeah. I got the message. I'll be there. Seven thirty, tonight." His voice sounded as if he were coming close to where Grace and Declan hid.

The closet door burst open and an arm reached in and snagged the bag of dry-cleaned clothes.

Grace froze. All Moretti had to do was look to the right and he'd see her as plain as day.

His arm retracted without him having leaned in far enough to see the two people hiding inside.

Still, Grace didn't move. She leaned against Declan, her body melting into his. She had no desire to move—*desire* being the key word in the scenario. Being this close to the man made her body come alive, as if it was waking up from a long sleep. Her skin tingled where he touched her, and her core coiled and heated, sending warmth throughout her body.

"I think he's gone," Declan whispered against her ear. His breath stirred the loose tendrils of hair brushing across her neck and made her shiver with the strength of her awareness.

"It's okay," he said softly, his deep voice resonating in his chest.

Grace wasn't so sure she was okay. She'd never felt quite so viscerally attracted to a man before. Not even her husband when they were together at the honeymoon phase of their marriage.

What was it about Declan that made her forget she was hiding in a closet in a building she'd entered illegally? Her gut told her to turn in his arms and see what happened next.

"Grace?" As if reading Grace's thoughts, Declan turned her in the circle of his embrace. "Are you okay?"

She stared up at him in the limited light from the open door of the closet. "I d-don't know."

"You're scared." Declan swept a strand of her hair out of her face and tucked it behind her ear.

Electricity fired across her nerves where his fingers brushed against her skin. She drew in a sharp breath, her gaze going to his lips.

"We'll get through this together," he whispered and bent to kiss her forehead.

"We will?" she said, her voice gravelly.

He smiled. "We will." Then he touched his lips to hers. "I promise."

Grace's knees turned to liquid. If Declan hadn't been holding her around her middle, she would have melted to the ground in a puddle of goo.

Never in her life had she been this incapacitated by a simple, meaningless kiss. And it scared the stuffing out of her.

She couldn't let a man have that kind of effect on her. Marriage to Mitchell had been hell. Divorce had been her only option to get away from his mental and physical abuse. She would never let a man control her again. Ever. No matter how tempting.

Grace straightened and pushed away from Declan. "We need to go."

"Were you able to get into the computer?"

"Sorry. I couldn't figure out his password."

"No worries. Let me try one more thing." He gripped her arms and gently moved her to the side.

Grace inhaled deeply, her breasts rubbing against his fingers around her arms, setting off sparks of fire.

What was wrong with her? Her friend was missing, they were basically breaking and entering, and she was lusting after a man she'd met less than twenty-four hours ago.

Declan left the confines of the closet, hefted the big box up from the floor and headed toward the exit. "Go to the elevator and press the down button."

"But—" Grace didn't like being separated from Declan. They were a team. At least she felt like they were a team. And she also felt safer when he was around.

"I'll be okay. If I'm not there by the time the car arrives on the floor, go down, leave the building and campus. I'll meet you back at the parking lot." He handed her the keys to her SUV. "Wait for me there."

When she hesitated, he gave her a gentle smile. "What I do next is better done without worrying about what's happening to you. If you're out of the building, I can move more freely. I can run for an exit, if I have to. Now, please. Go."

He didn't wait for her to agree or disagree. He left the office and strode into the bank of cubicles. "Is there a Riley Lansing on this floor?" he called out.

Grace wasn't sure what he was up to, drawing attention to himself. But she didn't want to get in the way of his plan. She left the office, exited the Special Operations area and headed for the elevator.

Her heart raced and she strained to hear any sounds coming from the offices she'd just left.

She braced herself for the blare of an alarm going off, indicating the building had been invaded and all exits should be closed off.

With that thought in her head, she punched the down key for the elevator and waited, her breath caught in her throat.

As soon as the elevator doors opened, she gave one last glance down the hall, willing Declan to come running from the Special Operations area. When he didn't, she was forced to enter the elevator alone.

She prayed Declan would be okay. His boss, Mrs. Halverson, was a very wealthy woman. Even so, Grace wasn't sure Mrs. Halverson would be able to bail him out of jail for unlawful entry into a secure facility.

Chapter Six

Declan strode down one aisle of cubicles, calling out, "Delivery for Miss Riley Lansing."

"She's not in," a female voice said. A woman with bleached-blond hair leaned out of her cubicle, took one look at him and smiled. "Maybe I can help you?"

"I have a delivery for Miss Lansing. Do you know when she'll be back?"

The woman shook her head. "Not a clue. She lit out of here yesterday like her hair was on fire, and I haven't seen her since."

"Yesterday?" Declan glanced at the box.

"She has to sign off on the delivery. I don't suppose you know where I can find her?"

The woman shook her head. "No, but maybe I'll schedule another delivery. Will you be the one to bring it?" She winked at him.

Declan gave her a hint of a smile. "I doubt it. They switch up the drivers," he said, making it up as he went along.

A man in a polo shirt and dress slacks stepped out of his cubicle. "Are you looking for Riley?" he asked.

"Riley Lansing," Declan said. "Can you point to where she sits? This box is getting heavy." It wasn't, but it was as good an excuse as any to get someone to show him where Riley's office was.

"She has the office near the back." The man in the polo shirt pointed to the wall behind him.

Declan strode past the man as if he belonged in the Special Projects area. He'd made it to a cubicle by the back wall with a placard bearing Riley Lansing's name when the polo shirt guy commented.

"I didn't know they allowed external deliverymen to bring boxes up here. I thought all packages came from our internal mail-room staff." He'd followed Declan to Riley's office.

"They were slammed down there and asked me to bring this up. It was marked urgent on dispatch."

"I guess it won't be as urgent, considering she hasn't bothered to show up today."

"But she was here yesterday? What, is she out sick or something?" Declan asked casually, setting the box on the floor. He took his time, his gaze scanning Riley's desktop for clues.

"I didn't see her, but she was here. Sometimes senior engineers work in the lab. She could have been in there."

"Are you sure she isn't in there now?" Declan asked. "Could you check to make sure? I can't leave the box without her signature."

Polo-shirt guy frowned. "I'm almost 100 percent sure she's not in there."

"Seriously, man. I can't leave the box without her signature." Declan raised his eyebrows. "Would you please go check?" *And get the heck out of here so I can look through Riley's desk.*

"Okay. I'll be right back." The man left.

Declan waited in the aisles until he turned down another corridor and disappeared out of sight.

Making certain no one else was watching, Declan searched Riley's desktop. He wasn't sure what he was looking for, but anything could be a clue. Papers were scattered around the surface as if she'd been working and left in a hurry. A notepad sat by the telephone. The top page was empty, but it had indentations from the person writing the previous note. He took the top page and shoved it into his pocket.

As he straightened, he noticed a shiny silver object on the floor. He bent to retrieve a charm bracelet. This, too, he shoved into his pocket.

"Like I thought, she wasn't there," a male voice called out.

Declan hefted the box up off the floor and smiled. "Thanks for checking. I'll take this back to the mail room. They can deal with it there."

"I could sign for it, if you like." The man in the polo shirt held out his hands.

"Sorry, it's supposed to go to Miss Lansing." Declan stepped past the man and strode the length of the cubicles, past the woman with the bleached-blond hair and out of the Special Projects area.

As he left the restricted area, two police officers and a security guard stepped off the elevator.

Declan lifted the box higher, blocking his face from view. He passed the group and was stepping onto the elevator when the security guard said, "Hey! You're not supposed to be up here."

Declan punched the button for the first floor and the button to close the elevator doors.

The security guard performed an about-face and started toward the elevator, but the doors closed before he could reach it.

Figuring the guard might call his buddies, Declan stopped the elevator on the third floor, punched the second-floor button and then exited. He found a bathroom, where he ditched the box and shucked the uniform shirt. He left the bathroom wearing the button-down cotton shirt he'd had on beneath the uniform.

He strode to the stairwell and walked the last two flights to the ground floor.

Several security guards stood in front of the elevator bank as the door to the elevator Declan had been on opened and a woman stepped out, a frown marring her face as she walked around the guards.

One of the security guards stepped into the

elevator as if he might find someone hiding in it.

Declan swallowed a chuckle and walked out of the building and through the gate. No one stopped him or yelled at him to slow down.

He walked slowly, though he wanted to sprint to the parking lot to make certain Grace was safe. As he neared where he'd parked the SUV, his stomach sank. The vehicle was gone.

Before he could react, a dark SUV pulled up beside him and a window rolled down.

"Get in," a female voice called out.

He turned to find Grace in the driver's seat of her SUV. He hopped into the vehicle and closed the door. "Why did you move the car?" he asked.

"I thought you might need me to be ready to make a run for it. Backing out slows one down."

He laughed. "You're getting good at this."

She shook her head. "I don't *want* to get

good at this." She left the parking lot and drove away from the Quest building. "What did you find?"

He dug the bracelet out of his pocket. "Do you recognize this?"

Grace frowned. "That's Riley's. She wore it to work yesterday morning."

"Are you sure?"

"I'm sure. I helped her put it on. She was in a hurry and the clasp can be tricky." She shifted her gaze back to the traffic in front of her. "Where did you find it?"

"Under her desk."

"So, she was at work yesterday." Her eyes narrowed. "Why would her supervisor lie?"

"I don't know, but he should have gotten his story straight with the people she worked with. One woman said she left in a hurry yesterday." He pulled the sheet of paper from his pocket. "I don't suppose you have a pencil?"

"In my purse. I keep a mechanical pencil."

"Not sure that will work, but I'll try."

"Try what?"

"I found this paper on her notepad. I thought she might have scribbled a note before she left."

Grace nodded toward her purse. "Check in the side pocket. The pencil is in there."

Declan dug around in her purse, found the pencil and rubbed it over the note. At first, he couldn't see anything, but as he continued across the page, two words appeared.

GET OUT

Grace swerved and righted the vehicle. "Does that say what I think it says?"

"Get out," Declan said.

Grace's fingers tightened on the steering wheel until her knuckles turned white. "What's happened to you, Riley?" she whispered.

"One thing we know for certain, Riley was at the office yesterday and her supervisor didn't want the police to know it."

Grace's lips tightened. "Why?"

"I don't know. But we know where he'll be at seven thirty, tonight."

Grace shot a glance at Declan. "We're going there?"

"You bet we are. Or at least I am." He tilted his head. "It might be better if you don't go."

Grace slammed her foot on the brake and glared across the console at Declan. "Why the hell not?"

Declan was glad he'd fastened his seat belt or he'd have been halfway through the windshield. "I get the feeling this might get dangerous."

"Riley's out there somewhere. If she's in danger, I'll do anything to help."

"Including putting yourself in danger?"

"Damn right, I would." Grace's eyes welled. "She's my friend. Practically family."

A horn honked behind them.

"The light's green," Declan said softly. "You want me to drive?"

"No," Grace said. Then she wiped her eyes

and hit the accelerator a little too hard. The SUV leaped into the intersection. "I'm okay. I just want Riley to be okay."

"I get that."

"We have several hours until the meeting this evening. Where should we look next?"

Declan glanced around. "We could retrace Riley's route she would have taken to the apartment and see if we can find any clues to her whereabouts."

"I did that last night into this morning."

"And?"

Her lips thinned into a straight line. "Found nothing."

"Does she have any places she hangs out when she doesn't want to go the apartment? Maybe she's afraid to go to the apartment. If she left on her own yesterday, she might be running from someone."

Grace concentrated on driving for a few moments before answering. "There's a coffee shop a couple of blocks from our apartment.

They have Wi-Fi. She goes there occasionally because she likes their coffee."

Declan folded the note and tucked it into his pocket. "Then let's hit all her normal haunts, get a late lunch/early dinner and be ready when Moretti goes to his meeting."

GRACE DROVE THROUGH the congested traffic to the coffee shop near their apartment. By the time they arrived, she needed the coffee to steady her nerves. "There's a reason I take the train as much as possible. Traffic is awful. We usually walk from the apartment to the coffee shop."

"Let me drive from here."

She handed him the keys. "You're on."

"When did you move in?"

"Four months ago, I had a hard time finding steady work paying enough to afford an apartment on my own. Riley offered to let me live with her until I got something that paid enough. I've been working for temp agencies, but I need to find a full-time job with benefits."

"Thus the interview with Mrs. Halverson?"

Grace nodded and climbed out of the SUV. "What about you? I don't know anything about you. When did you start to work for Mrs. Halverson?"

"Last night."

Grace frowned. "After the kidnapping incident?"

"Yup," he said and walked with her into the coffee shop.

At the counter, he waited for her to order, then he got a coffee for himself.

"Black. No sugar or cream. Just plain black coffee," he said.

Grace laughed. "Most people come for the fancy coffee."

"Unlike them, I like coffee just the way it is." He took the cups from the barista and nodded toward a table in the corner. "It's from years in the military, grabbing coffee when you can get it. It wasn't always available. You took it any way you could. And that was usually black."

He set the cups on the table and held a chair out for Grace.

She wasn't used to someone holding her chair for her. Her ex-husband hadn't been as concerned about her well-being. This made Grace like Declan even more. So far he was nothing like Mitchell. That was a huge plus in his favor. She lifted her cup and sipped the steaming brew. "How many years were you in the military?"

Declan took his seat and lifted his cup before answering. "Eleven years."

"Eleven?" She tipped her head. "I would think you'd have stayed for the full twenty before getting out."

His jaw hardened and his eyes grew dark. "It wasn't my choice."

"Oh." She could tell he didn't want to talk about it, but she couldn't stop the questions.

"How does that work? Did they not let you reenlist?"

"I was discharged," he said, his tone implying she'd asked enough questions. "You said you have a picture of Riley on your phone. Could you bring it up? I'll take it to the barista and ask if she's seen your friend."

"Yeah." More questions burned to be asked, but Grace could tell she'd pushed too hard already. She found a picture of Riley she'd taken three days ago. She had been sitting at the dining table in their little apartment, her laptop open, staring at the wall, a bit of a wrinkle in her brow. Grace had snapped the picture and then asked her what she'd been thinking about.

"Nothing," she'd said. Then she'd captured Grace's gaze. "When someone asks you to do something you know is right but will cause you a lot of grief, do yourself a favor and tell them to go to hell."

At the time, Grace thought the comment

was odd and out of left field. "What do you mean?" she'd asked.

Riley had heaved a big sigh and then redirected her focus on the laptop screen in front of her. "Nothing. Never mind."

Grace had gone to bed thinking her friend had had a bad day at the office and that she'd be her usually cheerful self the next day.

Then she'd gotten up early and gone into work before all the traffic became too congested. Grace had gotten up to use the bathroom only to find Riley struggling to get her lucky bracelet on.

"Here." Grace handed the phone to Declan.

When his fingers touched hers, the jolt of electricity passing from him to her made her drop the phone before he had it firmly in his hands. It clattered to the tabletop.

Declan captured her shaking hands in his. "Are you okay?"

Grace nodded. "I'm fine—just a little unnerved by all that's happened." She would have pulled her fingers free of his big hands, but she liked how warm and rough his skin was against hers. She didn't want him to let go.

But he did. And he lifted the cell phone. "This is Riley?" he said, staring down at her roommate's image.

"Yes. She's pretty, isn't she?"

"If you like redheads with green eyes," Declan said. "I've always liked blondes with blue eyes."

Heat rushed into Grace's cheeks and warmth filled her chest. She was a blonde. The warmth faded. "I have gray eyes."

"Did I say blue?" He glanced up, his eyes wide, innocent. "I meant gray." Then he winked.

Grace laughed, albeit a little forced. "I used to go for the guys with black hair and brown eyes. They were so mysterious."

"Used to?" Declan asked.

"Until I married Mitchell."

"Mitchell's your ex, right? Not a new husband?" His look was one of horror. "Are you on marriage number two?"

This time Grace laughed, humor bubbling up inside. She hadn't laughed like that in a long time. "No. I'm not married. I'm very divorced."

Declan let out a relieved sigh. "Thank goodness. I'd hate to think I'd kissed a married woman."

That heat returned to Grace's cheeks. "Speaking of which… Why did you kiss me?"

He rose from the table, phone in hand. "Time to get back to work. We have a missing person to find." He walked to the counter and turned the full wattage of his smile on the barista.

He had the woman blushing as much as Grace was sure she had been over his statement that he preferred blondes.

Grace tried not to stare, but she couldn't look away.

Declan had broad shoulders, narrow hips and thick thighs. When he walked, he had a natural swagger that couldn't be hidden, and it made Grace's heartbeat go from zero to 122 in two seconds flat.

He showed the woman the phone. The barista tilted her head to the screen, brushed her hair over her shoulder, smiled and nodded.

Grace leaned forward.

Did the barista's nod mean she'd seen Riley? Or was it more flirting with the former marine? Not that Grace could fault the woman's taste in men. Declan had it all. Good looks, a killer smile and a body that would haunt any woman's daydreams and nighttime fantasies.

When Declan returned, he walked toward her with the grace of a tomcat on the prowl.

Grace's mouth went dry and her pulse pounded through her veins. She wet her lips, her gaze going to his naturally.

"She thinks she saw her last night."

"Thinks?"

"She knows Riley as a repeat customer. A woman who looked a lot like Riley—same height, build and hair color—came in last evening, wearing a baseball cap pulled low over her eyes. She ordered the same drink Riley orders and sat in the seat she usually occupies when she comes to the coffee shop to work on her laptop."

"Why isn't she sure it was her?"

"She didn't wait on Riley and she had another customer. She only saw Riley out of the corner of her eye."

"What about the barista who waited on the woman in the ball cap? Where is she?"

"*He* doesn't work again until the weekend. He was training last night and wouldn't know Riley from anyone else. He's new."

Grace inhaled and let her breath out slowly. "Riley might have been here last night." She shook her head. "Then why didn't she come home? And where did she stay?"

"She might not want to involve you in whatever made her leave her office in a hurry," Declan said. "She could be on the run."

"From who? What?" Grace stared into Declan's eyes. "She's an engineer, not a secret agent."

Declan took her hands in his and squeezed gently. "We might not know until we find Riley."

"She's got some explaining to do." Grace pressed her lips together and then softened, her gaze on the man's hands holding hers. "She must be really scared." She glanced at the pocket Declan had slipped the notepad paper into. "Why would she write the words *GET OUT* and then disappear? So far, I haven't heard of any others from Quest Aerospace Alliance being threatened or having gone missing. There hasn't been anything in the news. Riley's disappearance seems to be unique. No one else has vanished, as far as we know, from Quest."

"Could she have been working on a project someone wanted more details about?"

"Someone willing to kidnap her to get it?" Grace shivered. "She could have been. Again, she didn't talk about work. She has a top secret clearance. Not many people get one of those in the private sector. She could have been working on something important. I wish she'd told me more."

"What is interesting is that Riley was here yesterday. And the barista said she was alone."

"Not kidnapped or held at gunpoint," Grace said. "Which means she disappeared intentionally." Her gaze met his. "I hope our efforts to find her aren't putting her into more danger."

"Me, too."

Grace tightened her grip on Declan's hands, glad he was with her. Thankful Mrs. Halverson had assigned him to assist her in her search for her roommate. "Riley's on the run, hiding from someone. But who?"

"Maybe Moretti will lead us to the ones Riley is hiding from."

Grace glanced at the clock on the wall behind the counter. "We have a couple of hours to blow. Want to come to my place? I have your rucksack there and I have some leftover lasagna in the refrigerator."

"Sounds good to me. But I don't want to take your food."

"Nonsense. I always cook too much. I'm a firm believer in leftovers. That way I don't have to cook as much during the week."

"Good thinking. I grew up in a house where there was no such thing as leftovers. I was one of three brothers and a sister. My mother, to this day, says she doesn't know how she kept enough food on the table for all of us during our teen years." Declan smiled. "We tended to wipe out the refrigerator every third day. All of us were very active in sports. We burned a lot of calories. My mother was a saint. We were the sinners. I never knew how much she did for us until I had to do every-thing for myself when I joined the US Ma-rine Corps."

"Your mother sounds amazing. Is she still with you?"

"She and my father live out west. In Wyo-ming."

"That's a long way from DC."

He shrugged and released her hands. "I haven't been back home since I left the mili-tary."

"Why?"

"I'm not quite sure how to tell them I've been discharged from the US Marine Corps." He shook his head. "My father was so proud the day I graduated basic training. And when I was accepted into the Force Recon training, you'd have thought I'd hung the moon. Dad couldn't have been prouder."

"I'm sure your folks would understand that whatever got you discharged from your unit, you had to have good reasons."

"We thought so at the time," he said softly.

"We?" Grace searched his gaze for emotion. What had he experienced? What had been bad enough he was kicked out of the military? "Who else was involved?" When he let go of her hands, she reached out this time to comfort him and refused to let go.

He stared down where their hands intertwined, without speaking for a full minute. Then his lips twisted. "Five of my Force Recon team and I were processed out. Dishonorable discharges, all of us. For doing what we knew was right." His words came out tight, and his fingers squeezed hers to the point they were hurting her.

But she didn't utter a word, figuring the pain of his grip was nothing compared to the pain of losing the career he'd obviously loved and watching his fellow marines going down with him.

"I'm sorry," she said.

"Why? You didn't do anything wrong. We

did. We knew what we were doing and that it was against orders. But we did it anyway. We also understood the consequences." He pushed to his feet. "Now, if you're serious about those leftovers, we should get going. We want to be at the meeting location before Moretti arrives."

Grace rose and left the coffee shop with Declan. The more questions she asked of him, the more she wanted to know. But all in good time. Declan obviously didn't feel comfortable talking about the incident that had gotten him kicked out of the US Marine Corps.

She could wait. But it didn't stop her from wondering. The man seemed to be a straight shooter, one who would do anything for someone else. She couldn't picture him as a traitor to his country. What else would have constituted a dishonorable discharge from the military? Unfamiliar with military law, she didn't know. Soon, she would find out.

Chapter Seven

After a fully satisfying meal of lasagna and garlic toast, Declan thanked Grace and then drove them across town.

They stopped at a convenience store for some disguises—two baseball caps—and moved on to the Blue Gill Bar & Grill, where Moretti was scheduled to meet with someone for something. Who and what? He had no idea.

They settled into a booth at the far corner of the barroom, in full view of the entrance and exit, in case Moretti came from either direction.

The waitress took their orders and returned with two glasses of fizzy ginger ale. When she'd left, Declan cast a glance toward Grace. She'd grilled him about his prior service, and he found himself wanting to know more about this woman who'd taken on the task of finding her missing roommate with fervor and undaunted determination.

"You and Riley were roommates in college?"

Grace smiled. "For four years. We never knew our first semester together would start a life-long friendship. Even after we went our separate ways after college, we kept in touch. We led completely different lives. Like I said, I married and focused on my husband and his life. Riley focused on her career." Grace laughed, the sound flat and strained. "Perhaps I would have been better off if I had stuck to my career."

"How long were you married?"

"Five years."

"And how long have you been divorced?" Declan shook his head. "You don't have to answer. I'm just killing time until Moretti arrives."

Though Declan gave her the out, she didn't take it; instead, she answered, "A few years."

"I'm sure you had good reasons."

She snorted. "Some might not think so."

"Try me."

She hesitated a moment and then said softly, "I forgot who *I* was."

"One of those *I found myself* situations?"

"Kind of." She swirled the ice in her drink, staring at it as it circled inside her glass. "My husband always made sure I knew who he was and how important his life was to him. I spent all my time living up to his expectations of what a proper wife was supposed to be—an extension of her husband. She shouldn't have a thought of her own—one that was not put there from her husband's mouth."

His lips twitched. He could imagine Grace

standing up to her husband. "Let me guess… you had a thought and it pissed him off."

"Once I remembered I was a living, breathing human being with a brain of my own, I had many thoughts. Not all reflecting him and his ideals. When we weren't in the company of others, he would punish me for speaking out." Grace touched the tiny scar on her cheekbone. Until that moment, Declan hadn't noticed it.

His fists clenched. Any man who hit a woman wasn't a man at all. He was a coward with control issues.

The scar did nothing to detract from her natural beauty. But he was certain it caused her more pain through her memories than it did when the injury had been inflicted.

"He made me feel like I deserved it," she said. "I embarrassed him in front of his colleagues."

Declan reached across the table and brushed his thumb along her cheek. "No man has the right to hit a woman. If you were mine, I would never raise a hand to you." He dragged his knuckles across her jaw and down the side of her neck. "I'd treat you with the respect you deserve."

Grace leaned her cheek into his open palm and stared into his eyes. "A girl could get used to hearing words like that, but what would it buy her? Maybe a few years of happiness, then more years of pain."

"Not all men are the same. Not all of them cause pain." He wanted to reassure her that his words were truth, but he wasn't in a position in his life to guarantee that assurance. He was, more or less, a marked man. On any job application or background check, his dishonorable discharge would come up. If not for Mrs. Halverson, he'd be homeless and jobless. Out of the goodness of one wealthy woman's heart, he wasn't completely destitute. For now. "And now you know who you are and what you want out of life."

"I'm me. For better or worse. And I know I want to be in control of my own destiny. I never want any man to control me ever again. Beyond that, I'm still trying to figure out what it is I'm going to do in this life. I seemed to have missed the career opportunities of a fresh college graduate. But I'm not going to let that stop me." She gave him a tight smile. "Enough about me. What was so bad that the military thought you couldn't be given a second chance?"

She'd come out of left field with the question. He'd been so engrossed in her story, he wasn't ready with a canned answer. How did a man tell a beautiful woman he'd practically committed mutiny?

GRACE FIGURED SHE'D pushed again. But after baring her soul to the man, he should reveal a little more about himself to her.

Declan opened his mouth and then shut it, his gaze going past her, his jaw tightening.

"Moretti just walked through the door," he said, his voice low but intense.

Grace fought to keep from spinning around to stare at Riley's supervisor, the man who'd lied to the police and to them. Why was the man hiding the fact Riley had been to the office that morning? Did he think he'd get away with it? Already someone from his own office had refuted his story.

Willing herself to remain facing Declan, Grace pleated the napkin in her lap and waited for Moretti to pass their table so she could watch his every move.

Her curiosity wouldn't let her just wait. She had to know. "What's he doing?"

Declan smiled at her, though his gaze angled over her shoulder to the man at the entrance. "He stopped at the door to look at his phone. Apparently, he just received a text message."

"Do you think he'll recognize us as the people he met at his office?" Grace asked.

Declan's lips twitched. "Not with the ball cap. It shadows your face nicely."

"As does yours." Grace smiled. He really was nice to look at. And reassuring, just being there. She couldn't imagine finding Riley on her own. "Thank goodness there's something for everyone in today's convenience stores."

Moretti strode by and took a seat in the farthest, darkest corner of the barroom. He lifted a menu and propped it up so that all that could be seen of his face were his eyes. And they were wide and watching everyone who came into the Blue Gill.

"He's awfully nervous." Grace lifted her glass to her lips and took a sip.

"Yeah?" Declan's eyes narrowed. "What's he doing now?"

She chuckled. "Hiding behind his menu and watching the door. Anyone interesting coming from that direction?"

"Nothing so far." Declan took her hand and

rubbed his thumb across her knuckles like a man who was showing affection to his date.

Grace sucked in a breath and held it. Declan's fingers were doing crazy things to her insides. And they were only touching her hand. She could imagine how sensuous they'd feel on other parts of her body. With considerable effort, she dragged her attention back to Moretti, afraid to look away for too long should he get up and leave without her knowing.

He was still there. Still looking over the top of his menu.

"Hmm." Declan's fingers tightened on hers. "My gut says the people who just walked in are interesting."

"Should I look?"

"No, keep your eyes on Moretti. Any reaction from him over the newest arrivals?"

"He just ducked behind his menu completely. All you can see are his hands."

"Like I said…interesting."

"How many?"

"Three. And they look like Mafia thugs."

"Holy hell," Grace said. "I need to see this." She swiveled in her seat and raised her hand, as if summoning the waitress.

Three big guys stood just inside the door. Each had dark hair, ruggedly angular faces and fists like ham hocks.

The waitress nodded at Grace and raised one finger. "I'll be with you in just a minute." She walked to the men at the door and offered to seat them.

They shoved her aside and stalked through the barroom, the leader's dark brow low on his forehead.

At that moment, Grace's cell phone jingled with the tone she'd assigned to incoming texts. Giving only a perfunctory glance at the screen, Grace didn't want to take her attention away from the drama about to unfold. But the words on the screen made her do a double take.

GET OUT!

The hairs on the back of Grace's neck stood at attention. The text had come from an unknown number. She stared at it for a moment and then passed the phone to Declan. "What do you make of this? It's the same message Riley had written on her notepad."

The jingle sounded again and another text came through.

Declan held the cell phone in his hand this time.

GET OUT NOW!

The three big guys chose that minute to pass their table, heading for the corner where Moretti hunkered low behind his menu.

Declan pushed to his feet, grabbed Grace's hand and yanked her out of her chair.

"What are you doing?" she said softly.

"I'm getting you out of here so that I can ravish your body," he said and waggled his brows. "The sooner the better." He didn't wait for her response, but tossed cash on the table and then half led, half dragged her out of the bar and into the street.

As soon as they cleared the door, gunshots rang out behind them.

Declan pulled Grace to the side of the door and pressed his body over hers, sandwiching her between himself and a brick wall.

With her face pressed to his muscular chest, Grace couldn't see anything. Her heart raced and her hands circled his waist, holding him close. Whoever was shooting hadn't run out of ammunition yet.

Declan lifted his head and glanced around. Shielding her body with his, he walked her to the entrance of an apartment building, opened the door and shoved her inside. He pointed at her. "Stay."

Grace grabbed his finger and glared at him. "I'm not a dog. You can't tell me to stay."

"Please stay," he amended. "I don't want you to be caught in the crossfire."

When he turned and started to walk out of the apartment entrance, she grabbed his arm. "Where do you think you're going?"

"Back to see if I can help."

"Help who?" Grace said. "Moretti? The Mafia? You're not even armed, are you?"

He pulled a handgun from beneath his jacket. "Charlie loaned me this."

Grace reeled backward, shocked that he'd been carrying the weapon throughout the day and she hadn't known he had it. "Are you even licensed to carry?"

"I am…was…before I was discharged from the army."

"Do they revoke licenses to carry from people who are discharged from the army?"

"I don't know," Declan said. "But I have it if I need it." He replaced it in the holster beneath his jacket. "I'm going back in. There are other people in there who might need help."

"Then I'm going with you," Grace insisted.

Declan shook his head. "It's too dangerous. You're not a trained soldier. I am."

"And don't most trained soldiers have buddies to cover their sixes?" She lifted her chin. "I've watched all those special-forces movies. I know you're supposed to have someone cover your back. Well, I'm your buddy. I'll cover your back."

"And you're armed?" Declan challenged.

Grace dug around in her purse and pulled out a Taser. "This is my weapon. And I'm not afraid to use it."

Declan frowned and glanced over his shoulder. "I need to go back in there. But I don't trust that you'll stay out of harm's way."

"Damn right I won't." She pushed past him. "Come on. The longer we wait, the more chance someone is getting hurt."

Declan snatched her hand and pulled her behind him. "You can't cover my back if you're not behind me. At least stay low and well to my rear until I figure out what's going on. Promise?"

He held on to her hand, refusing to let her move until she agreed.

"Okay," she said. "I promise to stay back behind you."

After another second, Declan moved, jogging back to the entrance of the bar. The sound of sirens wailed in the distance. "I'm going in. Stay out here and let me know if any other bad guys show up. And when the police get here, let them know there are innocent people inside."

"But I'm your backup. I should go in with you."

"Seriously, I need to go in first and make sure it's safe."

"And if it's not, and they shoot you, how am I to know?"

"Hell, Grace, if I'm worried about you, I'll get myself killed."

She clamped her lips shut on the words she

was about to say. He had a good point. "Okay. I get it. I don't want to distract you from doing what you do best." She flung her arms around his neck and pressed her lips to his in a brief, hard kiss. "Concentrate on staying alive."

He nodded. "I will, if I can have more of that."

"Incentive, man. There's more where that came from, but you have to come out alive to collect." She winked and stood to the side of the door into the bar that had gone eerily quiet. "Be careful."

"I will." Declan dove into the bar.

Grace counted to ten, feeling like a child playing a dangerous game of hide-and-seek. At ten, she still hadn't heard anything from inside, and she could barely breathe.

Letting the air out of her lungs slowly, she pushed back her shoulders, ducked low and slipped through the entrance. Using the techniques she'd learned from cop movies and reality television, she moved quickly to one side and crouched in the shadows.

Soft sobbing sounded from behind the bar. Two men lay on the floor behind an over-turned table, peering out from the sides of the tabletop.

Grace's gaze went to the far corner, where Moretti had been hiding behind his menu. The corner was empty, and Moretti, the Mafia thugs and Declan were gone.

The bartender rose up from behind the counter, a full bottle of unopened white wine held in his hand like a hammer.

The waitress crawled out from under an overturned chair, her mascara running in dark lines down her cheeks, her eyes red-rimmed from crying. She sniffed and looked around. When she spotted Grace, she whispered, "Is it safe to come out?"

"I don't know. Where did the big guys go?" Grace asked.

The waitress pointed. "Through the back door."

Grace hurried toward the rear of the building, her pulse thumping through her veins, her knees wobbling. Where was Declan? Surely he hadn't chased after the bad guys. They outnumbered and outgunned him three to one.

The rear emergency exit stood open. Grace eased up to the door and stuck her head around slowly.

The alley behind the bar stood empty, but for the big trash bin.

Her heart fluttered. Grace saw no sign of the Mafia brothers or Declan. It was as if they'd disappeared entirely. Had Declan surprised them as they got into their escape vehicle? Would they have knocked him unconscious and taken him with them? If so, would they kill him and dump his body in the Potomac?

She stepped out of the building and walked toward the corner. As she passed the trash bin, a faint sound caught her attention. She stopped and strained to hear it again. A groan sounded from inside the bin.

Grace leaned over the top and peered inside. The smell of rotting food and moldy trash hit her first. Then something moved among the boxes, bottles, cans and leftover food.

She pulled her cell phone out of her purse, hit the flashlight icon on the screen and shined the light down into the refuse.

Moretti lay among the trash, his body covered in blood.

The shock of her discovery made her stomach roil and bile rise up her throat. She stepped away from the bin and glanced down at her cell phone, her hand shaking so badly, she could barely function. Then she dialed 911 and gave her location. "There's a man with multiple gunshot wounds in the trash bin behind the building."

The dispatcher told her to seek safety until the police arrived. They already had an ambulance on the way.

By the time she finished the call, police officers emerged through the back door of the bar, weapons drawn.

Grace raised her hands. "I'm not armed. But there's a man in the bin. I think he's still alive."

An officer pulled her aside and frisked her. When they were certain she wasn't carrying a weapon, they made her go back through the bar and stand out on the street, in the midst of several squad cars. Still Declan hadn't returned.

The ambulance came and the EMTs loaded Moretti onto a gurney and carried him away to a hospital. Grace had about given up on Declan when she spotted him standing on the periphery of the small crowd gathering around the crime scene.

Her joy at seeing him surprised even herself. Afraid the police would pull Declan in for questioning and discover he had a weapon on him, Grace didn't rush over to see him.

She asked the officer in charge if they needed her anymore. They had her information and knew how to get in touch with her.

The officer told her she could leave as long as she remained in town in case they needed to ask her more questions.

Finally, Grace left the center of the investigation and walked away from the bar to where they'd left her SUV a couple of blocks away, in a paid parking lot.

Declan was there, waiting for her.

Grace walked straight into his arms.

He engulfed her in his embrace and held her for a long moment.

She inhaled the warm, musky scent of his aftershave and ran her fingers across the hard plains of his chest. He really was there. He hadn't abandoned her.

"I told you to stay out front." He smoothed the hair back from her forehead and pressed a kiss there.

"It was so quiet. I couldn't stand outside, not knowing what was happening."

"I see they found Moretti. Where was he?" Declan asked.

"In the trash bin behind the building." She leaned back and stared up at him. "Where were you?"

"When I went into the bar, I saw that Moretti and the thugs were gone. Since we came out the front and they didn't, I figured they'd exited out the back. I ran through and got to the back door as a dark SUV pulled away. I thought they might have taken Moretti. I wanted to get a license plate number so we could trace the vehicle, so I ran after it."

"You ran after their getaway vehicle?" Grace laughed and shook her head. "Are you crazy?"

He ran a hand through his hair, retaining his hold around her waist with the other hand. "Yeah. I am a little crazy." He drew in a deep breath and let it out. "They weaved through the streets. I knew I couldn't catch up with them by running behind them, so I cut through some alleys and side streets. I almost caught up when they got onto a main road and sped up." He sighed. "I lost them."

"Did you get the license number?" Grace asked.

His lips twisted. "No." He nodded in the direction the ambulance had gone. "What about Moretti?"

"The EMTs got him out of that trash bin and took him in the ambulance, but I don't know how he is. He was a bloody mess, with multiple gunshot wounds. I'll be surprised if he lives."

"Think we can get into the hospital to ask him some questions?"

"The man is possibly dying."

Declan raised his hands, palms up. "Haven't you heard? Dying men tell no lies."

Grace shook her head. "That's dead men tell no lies. I asked the ambulance driver which hospital they were taking him to. We could at least get a status on the man."

"And if we play our cards right, I can slip past security and ask him about Riley." He brushed her arm with the back of his knuckles.

His touch set off a flock of butterflies in Grace's belly. She swallowed hard and lectured herself on falling for a stranger. Declan was making it entirely too easy. "You don't give up, do you?"

His smile slipped. "Not when it's important."

Grace nodded. "We'd better get going. Moretti might not live long enough for us to get any information out of him."

"Now you're talking." He lifted her hand and pressed a kiss into her palm. "Let's go." Then he opened the passenger door and held it while she slipped in. He rounded the front of the vehicle and slid behind the steering wheel.

Grace keyed the name of the hospital into her cell phone's map application and brought up the directions.

They arrived several minutes later and pulled into the parking lot of the emergency room. Grace and Declan got out and walked to where the ambulances unloaded patients.

Two police cars were parked nearby. An ambulance had just left the dock when another pulled in.

"Might be difficult getting in to see Moretti if he's still in Emergency," Declan said.

"I have an idea. I'll create a distraction, and you slip in." Grace hurried toward the ER entrance where they were wheeling an old woman through the sliding doors. "Excuse me, excuse me," she called out as if attempting to get the attention of the paramedics already inside the hospital.

Her real goal was the ambulance driver, a guy the size of a refrigerator, who stepped in front of her, his arms crossed. "I'm sorry, ma'am, you can't enter the ER through the ambulance entrance, you'll have to go through the ER reception."

"But that's my grandmother. I have to stay with her."

"Lady—" the man shook his head, his lips pressing together briefly "—you have to go through the other entrance. The receptionist will help you once you check in."

"But she raised me when my mother abandoned me. She's all I have!" She stood on her toes in an attempt to see past him to the woman on the gurney headed down the hall. "I promised I'd stay with her. She'll be scared."

"She's unconscious," the ambulance driver said. "You'll have time to check in with reception."

"Oh, my God. Grannie!" Grace dodged to one side.

The driver clotheslined her with a beefy arm, catching her in the throat.

Grace played it and dropped to the ground, clutching at her neck. She held her breath and pointed at her throat, mouthing the words *can't breathe*.

"Oh, come on," the ambulance driver said. "I didn't hit you. You ran into my arm." He bent and held out his hand. "Take my hand. I'll help you up."

Out of the corner of her eye, Grace could see the EMTs with the gurney had made it down the hallway with the old lady and Declan had circled wide, coming around the other side of the ambulance. He was about to step through the doors when the ambulance driver straightened and started to turn to where his teammates had gone.

Grace had to do something, or the man would see Declan slipping through the door. She reached out and grabbed the driver's hand, bringing his focus back to her.

He pulled her to her feet, his brow dipping low. "Are you all right?" he asked.

She would be as soon as Declan made it inside. Grace swallowed hard.

And Declan was inside, the door closing behind him.

Letting go of the breath she'd held, she nodded. "I think I'll be okay." She gave the driver a weak smile. "I'll just go in through the main ER entrance, like you said. I'm sorry I caused such a commotion."

"Don't worry." He patted her arm. "They'll take good care of your grandmother. I'm sorry I had to be so stern with you, but it's against policy to let unauthorized personnel in through the back door."

"I understand. You were just doing your job." Grace brushed the dirt off her clothes, turned toward the main entrance to the ER and left the ambulance driver to close up the ambulance and wait for his team to return.

Now all she could do was wait for Declan to resurface, hopefully with some clues or information from Moretti.

She fished her cell phone from her pocket and stared down at the messages she'd received prior to the shoot-out between the three Mafia guys and Moretti.

GET OUT

GET OUT NOW!

Who had sent the messages? Could it have been Riley? Had she been somewhere close by and seen the three men coming in? Or was it the people who'd warned Riley to get out of her office?

The more Grace learned, the more she realized she didn't know.

She prayed Declan would find out something from Moretti. If not, they had very little to go on and still had no idea where Riley was. One thing was clear: if what had happened to Moretti was any indication, Riley was in danger.

Chapter Eight

Declan slipped into the emergency room behind the men pushing the gurney with the
old woman. As soon as he could, he ducked
into what appeared to be a supply closet filled
with medical kits, gauze and surgical para-
phernalia. Hanging on a hook were two white
doctor smocks. He grabbed one and slipped
it over his clothes. Then he found some blue
shoe booties and a face mask and pulled them
on. His disguise complete, he stepped out of
the closet and almost ran into the EMTs on
their way out, pushing an empty gurney.

One of them gave him a chin-lift greeting.

Declan gave one in return and kept walking toward the exam rooms. He lifted the chart from the bin hanging on the wall outside the first door he came to and flipped it open. The name on the chart was Archie Cooper. He replaced the chart and moved on to the next door and chart. Rita Davis. The scent of antiseptic stung his nose and reminded him of the times he'd been laid up in a hospital with shrapnel or gunshot wounds. He hadn't liked being in a hospital. He'd done his darnedest to get the heck out and back to his unit as quickly as possible. He had an unfounded view that hospitals were places where people went to die. It didn't make sense, because he'd been in one and hadn't died. Many of his teammates had been in them and come out alive. The ones who'd died had left an indelible impression on him.

As he approached the next door, a doctor and nurse emerged. The doctor was giving orders to the nurse. The patient was to be moved to the OR as soon as the surgeon on call arrived. In the meantime, they were to give him blood and do their best to stabilize him prior to moving.

Before they could look up and see him clearly, he entered the door beside him and let it close.

When he turned, he found the old woman who'd been brought into the hospital when he and Grace had arrived. She had been put on oxygen and an IV. Her skin was pale and waxy and her breath shallow.

Memories flooded in on Declan. Until then, he hadn't thought much about when he'd come as a teenager to watch his grandmother die in a hospital. He'd loved his grandmother and had spent many days on his grandparents' ranch in Wyoming, riding horses, swimming in the creek and running wild. He'd never thought about death or dying until his grandmother had fallen, broken her hip and succumbed to pneumonia. She'd wasted away, going in and out of the hospital until her frail body couldn't take it anymore and she'd passed away.

He went to the woman and lifted her hand. "I hope you get better. Someone out there loves you and wants you to come home."

A loud beeping sounded from the next room. Over the intercom system, a woman's voice said, "Code blue. Code blue in room seventeen."

Footsteps sounded outside the room where Declan stood. He walked to the door and pushed it open enough to see the doctor and several nurses rushing into the room next to the one he was in.

Declan dared to step out. Everyone else was focused on the code blue and didn't notice him hovering outside the room.

The nurses and doctor worked over the man, desperately trying to save him. With so much blood spilled on the floor, the medical staff slipped in it.

After several minutes, the doctor shook his head. "It's no use. He's bleeding internally. He won't make it until the surgeon can get in there and plug all the holes."

The pulse monitor showed an irregular heartbeat and low blood pressure. As Declan watched, the man's heartbeat flatlined.

"Call it," the doctor said after a few moments passed.

One of the nurses recited the time of death. Another noted it on the chart. The nurses and doctor stood back as a man's life ended.

Declan turned and ran into a woman in scrubs.

She frowned, her gaze searching his person. "I'm sorry, do I know you?"

"No," Declan replied automatically. "I'm new here."

"And you would be?" The woman's brows rose.

"Leaving. I think I'm in the wrong department." He nodded and dodged her, heading for what he hoped was the exit into the ER reception area.

"Someone call security," the woman said behind him. "Stat!"

Declan picked up his pace, taking long strides without running. He reached a door marked Exit, hit the button on the wall and waited while the door swung open.

A security officer hurried toward him.

Declan met him head-on. "Oh, good. There's a guy back there causing problems. They need your help with him." He stepped aside and let the security guard enter the restricted area. As soon as the door closed behind him, Declan scanned the waiting area for Grace and he removed the mask from his face.

Her brow furrowed and then smoothed.

A shout from inside the restricted area spurred Declan to move. He tossed the mask into a trash receptacle, pulled off the booties on his shoes and shucked the white jacket. By then Grace had reached him.

"Time to go." Declan took her hand in his and walked toward the glass double doors. The sensor set them in motion. As the restricted door started to open, Declan and Grace stepped out into the open air.

"What happened in there?" she asked beneath her breath.

"I'll tell you when we get out of the parking lot." He pulled her hand through the crook of his arm and hustled her along. They had climbed into Grace's SUV by the time the security guard emerged from the hospital.

"Duck," Declan said.

Grace leaned forward, below the windows.

Declan followed suit, raising his head only enough so he could track the progress of the security guard.

The man he'd passed on his way out of the restricted area was joined by another man in a security uniform. They walked through the parking lot.

As they neared the SUV, Declan's hand hovered over the ignition switch. He was ready to start the engine and pull out of the lot.

"Anything?" the guard one aisle over called out, his voice muffled through the window of the SUV.

The man near the back of the SUV responded, "Nothing."

They both turned and headed back to the building.

Declan let go of a sigh of relief. He waited until the guards were inside before he started the engine and shifted into Reverse.

"What was that all about?" Grace asked, straightening in her seat.

"A sharp nurse figured out I didn't belong in the back and turned the guards loose on me." He pulled out onto the street and hit the accelerator.

She touched his arm. "What about Moretti? Were you able to get in to him?"

He liked how her hand felt against his skin. For a moment, it derailed his thoughts...but then he was back. "I was close. But he wasn't talking."

"No?"

"No." Declan's jaw hardened. "The emergency room staff were working on him."

"And?" Grace's eyes widened.

Declan shook his head. "He didn't make it."

Grace slumped against her seat. "Damn."

"Yeah." Declan's lips twisted. "We're back to square one." He scratched his chin. "Does Riley have a computer she uses at your apartment?"

"She has one she uses for social media, but she was never allowed to bring her work home, because it was top secret."

"Let's find that computer and see if it will shed any light on where she might be."

"I checked it out when she went missing,

but I could have missed something you might see. I hate to think Riley is out there, running for her life." Grace chewed on her bottom lip. "She must be terrified."

Declan nodded. "Especially after what happened to her boss."

"Do you think she knows about Moretti?"

"Not only do I think she knows, I think she's the one who sent that text at the bar. I don't think we would have gotten out unscathed if it hadn't been for whoever sent that text."

Grace snorted softly. "It had to be Riley. She's like that—thinking of others when she's in hot water."

"Let's look through her room and see if anything will give us a clue. Maybe she has a secret hiding place for stuff she doesn't want anyone else to find."

Grace frowned. "I'll feel awful going through her things. She values her privacy."

Declan reached out to take her hand and

squeezed it. "I think she would forgive you if it means saving her life."

ALL THE WAY back to the apartment, Grace tried to think of anything Riley had said that could clue her into what was going on. For the past couple of months, Riley had gotten quieter about her work at Quest. When Grace asked how her day had gone, Riley had always responded vaguely. Nothing she'd said seemed to stand out.

On occasion, she'd received calls at night and rushed to take them in her bedroom, saying it was something to do with work and she didn't want to disturb Grace. Who had she been talking to?

As Declan pulled into the apartment complex's parking lot, Grace glanced up at the window she knew to be the one into their living room. A shadow passed by the open blinds. "Look," she said, pointing to the window. "There's someone in my apartment."

Her heart sped and she threw open the door of the SUV. "Riley's back." She ran for the stairs and up to the apartment.

"Grace, wait," Declan called out, his footsteps pounding on the steps behind her.

"It's Riley," Grace said, the joy of finding her friend making a smile spill across her face.

"Wait," Declan said again as Grace reached for the door handle.

She hesitated when she noticed the door ajar.

Declan caught up with her in time to grab her around the waist and pull her back. "What if it's not Riley?" he whispered.

"Not Riley?" Grace asked, her brain unable to comprehend. Who else could possibly be in her apartment? She and Riley were the only ones with keys, besides the landlord.

Then it dawned on her—the part of the doorframe right beside the lock was splintered and broken.

Her pulse hammering for an entirely different reason, Grace backed into the strength of Declan's body.

He shoved her behind him, pulled his handgun from the holster beneath his jacket and nudged the door wider with the barrel.

The sound of something crashing to the floor made Grace jump. She clamped a hand over her mouth to keep from gasping aloud.

"Call 911," he said softly. "And stay here. Do. Not. Follow. Me. Do you understand?" He caught her gaze and held it until she nodded in compliance.

Then he was inside the apartment, ducking into the shadows.

Grace pressed her back to the wall and focused on the gap between the door and the doorframe. She hated the thought of Declan in the apartment with a potential killer. The burglar could surprise, injure or kill the former Force Recon marine. But she had a job to do. She dialed 911 on her cell phone and pressed it to her ear.

When the dispatcher came on, she spoke in a quiet voice. "I have an intruder in my apartment." She gave the address.

"Are you in the apartment now?" the dispatcher asked.

"No, I'm outside the door. Please," Grace begged, "send someone quickly."

"Miss, I need you to stay out of the apartment."

"I will," Grace said. Though, if she heard a commotion and thought Declan was hurt, she might have to revisit that promise.

"I have units on the way. Stay on the phone."

A shot rang out and a loud crash sounded inside the apartment.

"Sorry, I can't stay on the line. Shots have been fired." Grace leaned hard against the exterior wall, her knees shaking. "Get the police here, now!" She ended the call and braved a glance around the doorframe and into the living room.

Two men were silhouetted against the moonlight shining in through the windows, locked in what appeared to be a wrestling match for the handgun in one man's hand that was pointed at the ceiling.

The hand shook, and shook again. The gun fell from his grasp and clattered against the coffee table before hitting the carpet with a dull thud.

Then one man threw a punch into the other man's face.

Grace gasped, praying the man throwing the punch was Declan, not the other way around.

The men fell over the armchair and crashed to the floor.

Grunts and bone-crunching pummeling sounds rose from the floor.

Her view blocked by the couch, Grace eased into the apartment. She snatched a lamp from a table in the hallway, yanked the cord out of the wall and advanced on the pair rolling on the floor.

Sirens screamed outside the apartment.

Her courage bolstered by the arrival of the cops, Grace held the lamp over her head, ready to slam it down onto the intruder's skull.

The men rolled again, and this time, the man on top was unmistakably Declan.

Unable to help, Grace stood back, praying for the chance to take out some of her anger, frustration and fear on the burglar.

Then the man bucked, shoved Declan to the side and lunged to his feet. Instead of running for the door, he grabbed one of the metal-framed barstools and used it like a bat, swinging at the living room picture window.

As footsteps pounded up the stairs, the chair crashed through the glass.

With a desperate lunge, the burglar dove

through the window and fell two stories to the concrete sidewalk.

Declan and Grace ran to the shattered window and stared down at the ground below.

The man lay for a moment, unmoving. Then he drew his knees beneath himself and pushed to his feet.

Two policemen burst through the door, weapons drawn.

"Hands in the air!" one of them called out.

Declan and Grace raised their hands.

"The intruder went out the window. He's on the ground outside now." Grace stepped to the side and pointed at the window with one of her raised hands. "If you don't get someone on him now, he'll be gone."

The officer spoke into the radio mic clipped to his collar, asking for his backup to go around the end of the building.

"He's armed and dangerous," Grace added. "He tried to kill my...boyfriend," she added, stumbling over the word.

"Are you two all right?" the officer asked.

"I am," Grace said. She glanced toward Declan, running her gaze over him.

"Can we lower our arms?" Declan asked.

"I guess," the officer said.

Declan lowered his but then held them out.

Grace walked into them and he closed them around her.

"I'm glad he didn't hurt you." Declan pressed his lips against her hair.

"Are you kidding?" She laughed. "You appeared to have bitten off a little more than you could chew."

"I wouldn't say that. I'm fine." Declan squared his shoulders.

"Yeah, you're fine." Grace grabbed tissue from the bar and dabbed at the blood on his brow. "You might need stitches."

"I'll be fine." He turned and pressed a kiss to her palm. "You were pretty fierce with the lamp."

"I was going to clobber him—" Grace

nodded toward the lamp she'd set on an end table "—but he went out the window before I could."

The officer took their statements, making notes on a pad. "Anything missing?"

The intruder had gone through the apartment like a mini tornado, tossing cushions from the couch. Drawers in the kitchen were dumped on the floor, and flatware and cooking utensils lay scattered across the tile.

"I don't know," Grace said.

"When you get a chance," the officer said, "make a list of anything damaged, destroyed or missing and give that to the detective in charge of the case." An electronic crackle sounded from the man's radio. The officer in charge spoke into the mic. "Status on the perp?"

"We got him," a staticky voice came over the radio.

Grace's pulse increased. "They did? They caught him?"

The officer held up his hand and spoke into the radio again. "Take him to the station. They'll question him there."

"Can we question him?" Declan asked.

The policeman shook his head. "I'm sorry, but you'll have to leave it to the detective."

"But he might know something about my missing roommate," Grace said. "Why else would he be in our apartment? Why now?"

"I can't answer that, lady, but you can come to the station and ask the detective all these questions. I'm sure he'll be of more assistance." He scribbled something on a piece of his notebook paper, ripped it off and handed it to Grace. "Detective Romsburg will help you at the station at that address."

The EMT checked out the intruder and declared him fit to go to jail. The police officers loaded him into a squad car, finished documenting the incident, took pictures and left.

Grace and Declan closed the door behind

them and turned the dead bolt. It didn't hold since the doorframe had been damaged.

Tears stung Grace's eyes. "What has Riley gotten herself into?"

Declan pulled her into his arms and held her for several minutes, stroking her hair. "We'll find her. I'm sure she'll clear everything up."

When Grace had more control over her emotions, she squared her shoulders and leaned away from the strength of his broad chest. She wished she could remain in the comfort of his arms, but they had to find Riley.

"Based on the way we found everything, the intruder was looking for something. But what?" Grace walked around the apartment, setting it to rights, looking at things from a completely different perspective.

Declan helped her set the cushions back on the couch and stand a chair upright. They straightened the kitchen, tossing the flatware and cooking utensils into the dishwasher. Then they moved into Riley's bedroom.

"He must have just gotten started when we arrived," Grace said. "It doesn't appear as if he made it in here."

Grace walked around Riley's room, her gaze skimming across everything personal to Riley. She rummaged through Riley's dresser drawers, searching for anything that might provide a clue to what was going on. All she found were sexy underwear, yoga clothes and T-shirts.

Declan turned the mattress on her bed upside down.

"What are we looking for?" Grace muttered, running her hand inside the drawer and the underside of the dresser top, thinking maybe there was a secret pocket or lever.

"Documents, a key to a safe-deposit box, flash drives or any other objects Riley might have hidden."

As Grace turned away from the dresser, Declan settled the mattress in place and smoothed the sheets and blankets, giving them military-tight corners.

Grace smiled. "You can take the man out of the military, but you can't take the military discipline out of the man."

He shrugged. "You do something often enough, and it becomes a habit."

She nodded. "Find anything?"

"Nothing." Declan pulled open the drawer on the nightstand and dumped its contents onto the bed. Riley had everything from hand lotion, paperback novels and phone-charging cords to an optimistic package of condoms.

Heat flooded Grace's core, rose up her torso, into her neck and filled her cheeks. She spun away, pressing her palms to her cheeks.

Not that she had thoughts of making love with the rugged marine. No. They'd just met. Their focus was on finding her roommate. The roommate who kept a stash of condoms in her nightstand when she hadn't been dating in the months Grace had been in the apart-

ment. But it was like Riley to always be prepared.

"If I was Riley," Grace murmured, "where
would I hide something that no one else could
find?"

With a chuckle, Declan stood next to Grace
as she surveyed the room with narrowed eyes.

"Did she have a favorite jacket, a box of
collectibles—" he looked up "—a journal?"

Grace frowned. Each night, Riley had sat
in the living room, jotting notes into a brown
notebook. "Yes!" She hurried to the adjoining
bathroom. They'd searched the living room,
kitchen and bedroom. After a particularly
stressful day at the office, Riley liked soak-
ing in the tub. She kept magazines and novels on a stand near the bathtub, within easy
reach.

Under an engineering trade magazine,
Grace found the leather-bound book. "Got
it!" she called out and carried it into the bed-

room. Grace sat on the bed and settled the journal on her lap.

Declan sat next to her.

"I feel guilty looking into her personal journal."

"If it helps us help her," Declan said, "I'm betting she'll be okay with it."

"Agreed." Grace opened the journal, praying she'd find something in Riley's notes that would help her locate her roommate, or at least understand what was happening with Moretti and the project Riley had been working on at Quest.

The first few pages dated back almost a year and rambled on about a shopping trip Riley had taken to New York City.

Grace flipped a few pages, bringing the dates to eight months ago and Riley's assignment in the Special Projects area. She'd been excited that she'd been given the opportunity to work on a top secret project. She'd already been through the extensive background check in order to attain her clearance to work in the area.

Grace skimmed the pages going forward. Riley wrote about her excitement with the work she was doing without actually divulging just what the project was all about. She wrote about Grace moving in with her and how she loved having her friend back in her life.

Tears welled in Grace's eyes. She'd felt the same. Riley was the sister she'd never had. Having grown up the only child of older parents, she'd led a pretty solitary life up until she'd roomed with Riley. The four years they'd spent together had been some of the happiest of Grace's life. Based on Riley's notes, she'd felt the same.

Two months ago, her entries changed, became more stilted and her satisfaction not as complete.

"Look at this," Grace pointed to a passage.

Had an interesting lunch meeting today outside the office. Not sure what's going on, but I can tell it's not good. The people involved mean business.

"What do you make of this?" Grace asked.

Declan shook his head. "Could you tell she acted any differently at that time?"

"I don't remember. But she did start keeping to herself more about that time. I thought it was because she was working so hard at the office, she didn't have time to spend with me. I didn't push it, giving her space to get the job done."

Grace kept reading.

I don't know how long I can keep going like this. Someone is going to figure it out and come knocking. I don't feel safe anymore.

"Figure out what?" Grace asked. "What were you doing?" She couldn't believe her friend had been worried and suffering all this time and she hadn't known a thing about it.

I'm going to tell them I want out. I can't do this anymore. Living this lie is making me jittery. I can't sleep. I'm looking over my shoulder all the time. I don't have anyone to talk to about it. It's getting more dangerous with each passing day. But I still don't know who is behind it. Until I do, I'm stuck in this mess. Why did I let myself get into this situation?

Grace gripped the book. "Why didn't she talk to me? I've been here."

"Maybe her problem was with the project she was working on. You said she couldn't talk about the project because it was secret."

"That's what she said." Grace pressed her lips together. "I should have dug for more information. I was so caught up in trying to find a full-time job, I didn't consider Riley might have problems. I thought she was just pushing to finish her project and gave her room to think and work."

Declan slipped an arm around Grace's shoulders. "You thought you were doing right by staying out of her way so that she could concentrate."

Grace flipped to the next page.

I hate that I'm scared all the time. I wish whoever he is would show himself so they can do something about the situation. I can't take this much longer. I told them I wanted to quit and they said I couldn't.

A shiver rippled along Grace's spine. "She was scared. Oh, Riley. I wish I had known."

Chapter Nine

Declan hated seeing the tears in Grace's eyes. She cared deeply about her roommate. That she would do anything to help her friend said a lot about Grace. She was a human being with a heart as big as the Wyoming skies.

He stared at the writing on the page of the book. "Who was the *he*—the one she wanted to show himself?" he asked, drawing attention back to the problem they both needed to solve.

Grace curled her fingers into a fist. "And who were the *they* who wouldn't let her quit?"

"Anything else in that book?" Declan asked.

Grace rifled through the rest of it, but the pages were blank and nothing shook loose. "That's all." She flipped to the back and stopped. "No, wait." On the last page was a number and the initials *SBOA*. She held the page up for Declan. "What do you think this might be? Anything?"

He studied it for a moment. "Could it be an account number and the initials of the business?"

Grace studied the initials and shook her head. "I have no idea."

Declan tapped his chin, trying to think what the numbers and letters meant. "Does she have any paperwork here in the apartment? A file of some sort?"

Grace nodded. "She has a small fireproof lockbox, where she keeps all her bills and legal documents."

"Where?" Declan asked.

"In the bottom of her closet." Grace leaped up from the bed and ran to the closet. She dove into the back, hauled out a laundry basket and some shoes, and then dragged out a heavy metal storage container the size of a one-drawer file cabinet. She sat on the floor beside it. "This is what she uses to hold all her legal documents and account information."

Declan tried to open the box, but it was locked tightly. "Any idea where she might keep the key?"

Grace's lips twisted. "On her key chain. The one she probably had with her when she disappeared."

"Does she have a spare set?" Declan asked.

Her eyes narrowing, Grace tilted her head. "I think so. Now, where did she keep them?" She glanced around Riley's bedroom and shook her head. Then her eyes widened. "The kitchen. She keeps a spare set of keys hanging on a hook in the pantry." Grace hurried past Declan and out into the living room.

Declan followed close behind.

When Grace reached the kitchen, she pulled open the door to the small pantry. On the inside panel of the door was a set of hooks. One had a key chain with a bright red plastic heart and several keys on it.

Grace snatched the chain from the hook, spun around and walked straight into Declan's chest.

Declan wrapped his arms around Grace's waist to steady her.

She rested her hands, keys and all, on his chest, her eyes rounded, her breathing ragged. "Oh, I'm sorry... I didn't know you were there."

"It's okay." He stared into her beautiful eyes, captured with how clear and gray they were. For a long moment, he stood with Grace in his arms, unwilling to move and break the spell she held him under.

Then she swallowed and raised the hand with the keys. "I found it." Her voice was no more than a breathy whisper, drawing attention to her mouth and her pale, rose-colored lips.

Before he could think about what he was doing, Declan bent and brushed his mouth across hers. When he realized what he'd done, he reached for the key ring and set her to arm's length. "My apologies. I don't know what got into me. No, that's wrong. I do know what got into me. But it doesn't make it right." He turned and walked back into the bedroom, surprised Grace hadn't accused him of taking advantage of her with that unexpected kiss. He wouldn't be surprised if she told him to leave and never come back. He'd overstepped the boundaries of his position more than once.

For that matter, what was his position when it came to Grace? He was there to help her find her roommate. But she wasn't his boss. Charlie was his boss. What did that make Grace? His partner? What did it matter? He had a job to do. Find Riley. Nowhere in that job description was the task of seducing Grace.

But he wanted to.

Boy, did he want to. When his arms circled her body, he had to fight his natural urge to tighten his hold. And he'd lost that struggle when he'd kissed her.

Hell, he had to remember he was damaged goods. Nothing he could do would erase the black mark on his military record. It would follow him around for the rest of his life. Anything he did would be tainted with that mark. And he'd been so very proud of his job, his connection with the US Marines and, most of all, his position on Force Recon.

He had nothing to offer a woman like Grace. Not a home, nor a bankroll. She deserved someone with a clean record and an unsoiled past.

He selected the bright silver key on the key ring, slipped it into the lock on the box and twisted it with a little more force than necessary, angry at himself, the situation and the injustices of the world.

The lock opened, but he hesitated, his breathing ragged, his heart pounding. The one little kiss reminded him of all he'd given up when he'd made the decision he had back in Afghanistan.

Would he do it again?

Hell, yeah.

Then he had to accept it and move on. Without Grace.

A hand on his shoulder brought him back to the task before him. "Are you all right?" Grace asked.

"I'm fine," he said through gritted teeth. He swung open the door and pulled out a drawer with neatly arranged files in alphabetical order. He thumbed through to the *s* tab, where he found several receipts from businesses starting with the letter *s*. He kept moving through the file until he reached a folder marked Signature Bank of America.

He checked the number on the account against the number on the page in Riley's journal. They didn't match.

"Apparently she banks there, based on the statements," Grace said. "But why would she have a different account number?"

Then it struck Declan. "Could it be the number on a safe-deposit box?"

Grace frowned. "Why would she have a safe-deposit box?"

"Most people put things of value in a safe-deposit box. Something they don't want lost or stolen," Declan said.

"Do you think whoever broke into the apartment might be looking for that something?" Grace asked.

"Maybe." Declan dug into the SBOA file and located a sealed envelope. "I'd ask if she'd be mad if I was going through her things, but I think we're way past that now." He ripped open the envelope and found a sheet of paper and a strange heavy key with a number engraved on the side. The number matched the one written in the back of Riley's journal. "Bingo."

Grace drew in a deep breath. "Doesn't Riley have to be the one to get into her own safe-deposit box?"

"Yes. Unless you have permission to enter the box." Declan held up the sheet of paper.

Grace leaned over his shoulder, her long blond hair brushing against his cheek. "She created a power of attorney for me? How did I not know this? Why wouldn't she tell me?"

"Maybe she figured you didn't need to know," Declan guessed.

"Until I needed to know." Grace folded the paper and tucked it into the journal. She hugged the book to her chest and stared up into Declan's eyes. "What's next?"

"We go to the police station and see if we can get any information out of our burglar," Declan said.

"Well, we did come here for the laptop."

Grace pointed to a shelf by Riley's bed. "It's there."

Declan grabbed the laptop from the shelf. "You said there's nothing on it, but we'll take it with us if we don't get the answers we're looking for."

Grace nodded. "Too bad it's too late to go to the bank."

Declan gave her arm a gentle squeeze. "We can go there tomorrow."

GRACE WAS MORE than willing to let Declan do the driving. Declan found a piece of plywood near the apartment trash bin. He borrowed some wood screws and an electric drill from Mr. Miller, the neighbor in the apartment two doors down. In a few short minutes, he had the doorjamb fixed enough that they could lock the door and leave, feeling moderately sure no one would be able to get in easily. Not that there was anything else of any great value inside to be stolen, other than the television.

Nothing in the apartment was irreplaceable, except Riley.

A knot formed in Grace's throat as she sat beside Declan. She had no idea what she would have done without his assistance and support. She'd have been waiting by her telephone for the police to call. She would probably have been home when the intruder had entered her apartment.

Her hands shook as she held her purse with the journal and the key to the safe-deposit box inside. What would she have done if the intruder had caught her alone? Sure, she'd have fought tooth and nail to protect herself, but would it have been enough?

And what was Riley having to deal with? Was she being held somewhere? Or had it been Riley who'd texted her to get out of that bar when the three thugs had come in to get Moretti?

Hope had been fleeting when she'd thought Riley might be trying to protect them. Since that text, she'd heard nothing more. She'd even sent a text back to the same number, but received no response. Minutes later, the text had shown up as undeliverable.

In one day, her seemingly insignificant worries about finding a full-time job had morphed into life-or-death concern for her roommate and now herself. Whatever had frightened Riley into hiding might have put Grace into just as much danger. The people after Riley had killed her boss. If Grace had been home alone when the intruder broke in, she too might be dead. She had Declan to thank for sneaking into Riley's office with her, being with her at the bar and scaring off the intruder from her apartment.

She stared across the console of her SUV at the man driving. "I know so little about you," she admitted.

His lips twisted. "You've only known me a day. And vice versa."

Grace snorted. "Do we ever really know other people?" Her fingers tightened around her purse, which contained the journal that had revealed so much more about her friend than Riley had ever shared.

"What do you want to know about me?" Declan asked, his attention on the road ahead.

"Other than why you were booted out of the Marine Corps?" When he turned with a frown, she held up her hand. "You don't have to say unless you're ready. How about we start with something less damning, like what were you like growing up? Are you the youngest or oldest of your siblings, and what's your favorite song? We have at least five minutes at this stoplight, based on the line of traffic in front of us." She gave him a wry smile. "Go."

He sighed. "Like I said, I grew up outside Cheyenne, Wyoming. We lived on a small ranch with cattle, horses and wide-open ranges to run around on. I have one sister, Susan, and two brothers, Patrick and Daniel. Our parents are still alive and, like I'd already told you, they are probably wondering why I haven't contacted them since I got back from deployment."

"I can't believe you haven't let them know you're safely back from Afghanistan."

Declan's lips pressed together. "My father is a retired army infantryman. One of my brothers is an Air Force pilot and the other brother is army infantry like our father. My sister joined the navy as a nurse. Call me a coward, but I don't know how to tell them I was kicked out of the Marine Corps. I didn't want to go home with my tail between my legs." His hands tightened on the steering wheel, his knuckles turning white with the strength of his grip. "I had to find my way back."

"Based on Mrs. Charlotte Halverson, you have a job now. Isn't that enough?"

He shook his head. "I haven't proven myself yet." He shot a glance her way. "I haven't found Riley. As Charlie would say, I haven't made a difference."

"Charlie?"

He gave her a tight smile. "Charlie doesn't like me calling her ma'am."

Grace had met the woman and figured she was a force to be reckoned with. "After we find Riley, will you talk with your parents and let them know what happened?"

He nodded. "I love my folks. I just don't want to disappoint them."

And Grace could bet that Declan couldn't stand to see what he would expect to be the disappointment in their faces. If they truly loved him, which she suspected they did, they would not judge him and find him wanting. They would be ecstatic to have him home. They would understand whatever decisions he'd made and support him all the way.

But Declan had something to prove to them. No...to himself. He had to find his own worth and new path in life before he could go back home.

The light changed, and Declan drove on. Soon he pulled into the police station, where the officer in charge had indicated they'd taken the intruder.

Dusk settled over the city and streetlights flickered on.

Inside the station was a hub of activity. Men in uniform led lawbreakers past the front desk and into interrogation rooms and holding cells. Grace really had no idea how it all worked. She clutched her purse to her side and followed Declan inside, where he asked for the detective working the breaking-and-entering case at her apartment complex.

The desk sergeant scanned his computer, clicked the keyboard and frowned. "Are you sure they brought the suspect here?"

"That's what the officer in charge of the investigation at my apartment told me." Grace fumbled in her purse, her pulse beginning to race. "He said I could speak with the detective on the case, if I wanted more information." She gave up on her purse when she remembered where she'd placed the sheet of paper. Grace pulled the note the officer had given her out of her back pocket and handed it to the sergeant. "This is the address he gave me and the name of the detective. Detective Romsburg."

The desk sergeant stared at the paper and shook his head. "That's this address, but we don't have a Detective Romsburg."

Grace blinked. "No? Not now? How about in the past?"

The sergeant shook his head. "Not now or ever—that I know of. Not at this station or in this precinct, at least not for the past twenty years I've been here." He handed the paper back to her. "I'm sorry, miss, I don't have record of the break-in. We can't help you."

"But I placed a 911 call. You have to have record of that," Grace said.

"Address?"

Grace gave it, along with her phone number.

The sergeant frowned and clicked his computer keyboard. His frown deepened. "I have record of the call and then another call to cancel the request, saying the caller was mistaken."

"That can't be right. I didn't call back." Grace's head spun and she felt the blood drain from her face.

"Sorry, ma'am. That's all I have," the sergeant said.

Declan gripped her elbow and held her steady until the dizziness passed. "Thank you for your assistance, officer." He turned Grace and marched her out of the building.

"What's going on?" Grace asked as soon as they cleared the exit. "Why would that sergeant lie about the break-in?"

"He might not have been lying. The officer in charge at your apartment might have given you the wrong address. Let me get on the phone and see what I can find out. In the meantime, we're going to get you some food and take you back to your apartment for rest." He hooked her elbow and led her toward the SUV.

Grace dug her heels into the pavement. "But we haven't found Riley. We can't give up now." She knew she was being unreasonable, but her frustration level had maxed out. "I can't give up on her. She's all I have."

"Tell me about her on the way back to your place. Maybe we'll get lucky and she'll be there, waiting to fill you in on her latest adventure."

Grace frowned at Declan but let him lead her to the vehicle and help her inside. "You don't really think she'll be there, do you?" she said as he fastened her seat belt around her waist.

He smiled and pressed a brief kiss to her lips. "We can always hope."

The brief kiss had her head spinning even

more. How could she think straight when the man kissed her? And not for the first time. The first time had taken her completely by surprise.

What did it mean?

Nothing. Don't read anything into that kiss. He's just being nice.

And the kiss *was* really nice. His lips were soft but firm, warm and dry. And sexy as hell.

Declan slid into the driver's seat and paused before starting the engine. "I did it again. I'd say I was sorry, but I'm not. I can't help it. Every time I'm near you, I can't help kissing you. Tell me to stop, and I will." He finally glanced her way, his eyes a light blue. But it was his mouth Grace couldn't lose focus on. That mouth that made her lips tingle and her insides coil for more.

Grace touched her lips, pressing her fingers against them to stop the tingling. But the sensation wouldn't go away. "It's okay."

"No," he said and started the engine. "It's

not okay. I shouldn't kiss you. I'm supposed to be working for you to find your roommate. This isn't the time or place. Maybe I'm the wrong person for this job."

She touched his arm. "That kiss was more than okay. For that brief second, I felt safe and hopeful. Maybe it wasn't the right time, but I needed it." Grace dropped her hand to her lap. "I needed it," she whispered.

And she *had* needed that human contact. More than that, she'd needed a reminder that she wasn't alone.

Chapter Ten

Back at Grace's apartment, Declan made a few calls. First to the local police headquarters, describing what had happened and how they had been misdirected.

The police headquarters said they'd look into the incident and get back to them.

Not holding out much hope, Declan placed a call to his new boss, Charlie.

He still struggled with calling the older woman by her first name. But the more he did, the better she liked it.

"Have you found Grace's roommate?" Charlie asked.

"No, ma'am. I was wondering if you had any connections on the police force."

"As a matter of fact, my late husband was a big proponent of the local Fraternal Order of Police. We donated a lot of money to the survivors of police officers lost in the line of duty." She paused. "Why?"

Declan told her what had happened up to that point. "If you have any pull on the local police force, I could use a contact."

"I'll get one for you. I refuse to believe they lost the perp. There has to be a perfectly good explanation."

"Let me know when you find it," Declan said.

"What are you going to do next?" Charlie asked.

"I don't like that an intruder made it into Grace and Riley's apartment."

"You aren't going to leave Grace alone, are you?" Charlie asked.

"No. I'm staying with her tonight."

"Do you want to stay at my place? I have an excellent and very expensive security system."

Declan smiled. "I know. If things get even more dangerous for Grace, I might take you up on that offer."

"Please do. I hate the idea of another innocent person being hurt."

"Speaking of innocents, how are you?"

She snorted. "Like I'm an innocent. I'm staying put inside my wonderful security system until your guys arrive," she said. "I did venture out long enough to express my condolences to the families of my bodyguards killed in the skirmish yesterday."

"I'm sorry you had to go through that."

"I'm sorrier it happened to such good people. Their families shouldn't have had to suffer their loss. Those were good men, doing their jobs."

"Any word on what they had in mind by kidnapping you?" Declan asked.

"The FBI questioned the guys they captured. They're still not talking." She sighed. "I'm a rich woman. They probably hoped for a sizable ransom."

"Are you sure you don't want me there?" Declan asked. Not that he wanted to abandon Grace and Riley. Not now that he had so much effort invested in their welfare. But Charlie had been attacked and her welfare was important to him as well. He could take Grace to her place and keep them all secure.

"No. I'm safe behind my walls," Charlie said. "Your guys are on their way. They'll arrive tomorrow."

"Again, Charlie, thank you for having faith in me and my team."

"I wouldn't have offered to set up Declan's Defenders if I didn't believe you and your men were the ones to make it happen. Based on what you told me, you all made the right decision. Your commanders had to make the decisions they made, right or wrong. I'm sorry you had to leave the Marine Corps." She laughed. "I'm sorry for you. I can't say I'm sorry for me. If you hadn't been released from the marines at the time you were, and if you hadn't been on the street you were at the time you happened along, I might not be here today." She paused. "I believe some things are meant to happen for a reason. Call it divine intervention, fate or dumb luck. I don't care. I'm just glad you found me."

Declan's heart swelled. "And I'm glad you found me." He pushed back his shoulders. "Thanks for taking a chance on me. I'll do my best to prove I'm worthy of your trust."

The older woman chuckled. "Sweetie, you already have. But wait… What do you think about the name I've coined for your group?"

"What was that?"

"Declan's Defenders," Charlie said. "I'm all for alliteration."

"You should have named the organization after you. It was your idea."

She chuckled. "And I might have, but I couldn't come up with something satisfying that went with Charlie, other than Charlie's Angels…and well…that wouldn't do. So, unless you have an objection to it, Declan's Defenders it is."

"Thank you, Charlie. You're an amazing woman."

"I know. Now, bring Riley home safely."

"Will do, ma'am—Charlie." Declan ended the call and went in search of Grace.

The door to her bedroom was open, but she wasn't there. He heard the sound of the shower through the bathroom door.

His groin tightened.

When he'd held Grace in his arms earlier, he'd felt something special. Yeah, he'd held women in his arms before, but Grace was different. She was strong, yet vulnerable. And her body fit perfectly against his. She wasn't painfully thin like some women liked to be. The woman had curves and valleys and hips his mother would have called good for breeding.

As his thoughts turned to breeding, he let his imagination go down that path with Grace in mind.

Grace would bear beautiful children. Blond-haired, gray-eyed girls like their mother. They'd be kind, courageous and beautiful, just like Grace.

He didn't realize he'd been standing, staring at the bathroom door until the water shut off and he heard the sound of the shower curtain rings sliding across the curtain rod.

Declan left her bedroom door and hurried back into the living room. Grace didn't need to know he'd been having crazy daydreams about her babies. Babies whose lives he'd never be a part of.

When he'd been younger, before he'd joined Force Recon, he'd always thought he'd marry someday and have three or four children like his parents had. He liked kids and they liked him.

After so many deployments in which he'd gone into villages where innocent women and children were used as shields or forced to be weapons of war, he wasn't as certain. After all he'd seen, all he'd done, how could he feel right about bringing children into a world so broken?

Yet he'd stood in Grace's bedroom and thought about what it would be like to hold her baby in his arms. To make her pregnant with his child.

Declan groaned at the image conjured up of Grace naked in her bed, him driving deep inside her body, filling her with his seed.

And if wishes were horses…his mother would have said. Wishing got him nowhere. Action was what was needed. Inaction made him crazy. He stood in front of the boarded window overlooking the back side of her apartment complex. The drapes were drawn and a board stood in the way of his view, but he closed his eyes and imagined the trees he had seen earlier that day.

A soft hand touched his arm. "Hey. What are you thinking about?"

Declan flinched and took a step away. "Nothing."

"Sorry. I didn't mean to startle you." She wrapped the tie of a silky powder-blue robe around her middle and cinched it. "You were frowning. I thought maybe you were in pain."

He couldn't tell her he was in pain because he was thinking about making love to her. Hell, if she looked down, she'd see the evidence in the swell beneath the fly of his jeans.

"Were you thinking about your team?" she asked.

"No." At that moment, he was thinking about untying the blue robe and sweeping Grace up into his arms. He wanted to make mad, passionate love to the woman as he pressed her to the wall—the bed being too far away.

Declan took another step away.

Grace frowned and closed the gap. "Seriously, were you in pain?" She raised her hand to cup his cheek.

He grabbed her wrist and held it. "The only pain I'm in is when I touch you. Go to bed, Grace." He let go of her hand and again moved a step away.

Her eyes flared and her cheeks grew pink. "You were thinking of me?"

"Yes. Now, do us both a favor. Go to your room alone, close the door and sleep."

She shook her head. "I can't."

"What part can't you do?"

Grace inhaled a deep breath and released it before she spoke. "After all that's happened today, I can't go into that room alone. We don't know if the intruder escaped the police. He could come back. Logic tells me he wouldn't dare try again. But deep down, I don't trust that he'll stay away."

He started to reach for her, to pull her into his arms. He raised his hand halfway to her arm, stopped and let it fall back to his side. "I'm here. I won't let anything happen to you."

"You'll be in here, but I'll be in the other room. What if he hurts you? I'd never know until it was too late." She took another step closer. "It seems to me, we could protect each other. You know... I'll have your back and you'll have mine."

Declan closed his eyes, his hands all over her naked back in his mind. "No can do," he said.

She ran her tongue across her lips, making him exponentially hotter. "What if I leave the door open? Then at least I could hear if someone comes in." Grace went to him and laid her hand on his chest. "I could help you."

"I'm supposed to be helping you, not the other way around." Placing his hands on her hips was his first mistake. Getting lost in the depths of her pretty gray eyes was his second. "Don't you understand? I'm trying hard to keep my hands off you. And I'm failing miserably."

She curled her fingers into his shirt and inhaled deeply, her breasts brushing against his chest. "Then quit trying so hard." She leaned up on her toes and pressed her lips to his in a feather-soft kiss.

Declan groaned and his arms tightened around her middle. "Now you've gone and done it," he said against her mouth. Then he claimed her in a breath-stealing kiss that started out hard, almost punishing. He wanted to chastise her for making him lose control. But as the kiss deepened, she opened to him, letting his tongue slide past her teeth to take her in a long, silky caress.

She raised her hands to clasp the back of his neck, pulling him closer. Her hips pressed against his, the evidence of his desire nudging against her belly.

A moan rose up her throat and warmed his mouth. She wrapped her calf around his and rubbed the apex of her thighs across his thigh.

Past any kind of restraint, and hopelessly in danger of losing complete control, Declan swept Grace up in his arms and held her against him. "Now's the time to back out. Say the word and this ends here." How he'd stop, he wasn't sure. But he had to give her an out.

She cupped his cheek, her lips hovering over his. "I want you to hold me," she said. "All night long."

"Let's be clear. Hold you only?" He shook his head. "Can't promise you that."

"Then let me make myself crystal clear." She bracketed his face between her palms and stared into his eyes. "I want you to make love to me all night long."

Still he hesitated. "You're not concerned that we only just met?"

"I've never been more certain in my life."
Then she kissed him and pressed her body
closer.

Clutching her to him, he strode into her
room and stood beside her bed without breaking the connection. When at last they separated for air, he lowered her legs and let her
slide down his body until her feet touched
the ground.

Grace reached for the tie on her robe.

Declan brushed her hands away and loosened the knot.

She shrugged the silky robe from her shoulders and let it slide down her back and arms.
It slipped over her body to land on the floor
at her feet.

Beneath the robe, she wore a matching blue
baby-doll nightgown that teased the tops of
her thighs and left her legs completely exposed.

He groaned. "Do you even know what
you're doing to me?"

Her chuckle warmed his insides. "I have an idea." She reached low and cupped the bulge of his straining erection through the denim of his jeans. Then she grasped the button and paused. "I should feel guilty for wanting this when Riley is on the run, but I can't help it."

"*You* can't help it. I thought resisting kissing you was hard enough. This goes far beyond that."

She pushed the button loose and slid the zipper downward in an agonizingly slow movement. Finally, his stiff erection sprang free of the confines of his jeans.

Grace's mouth curved upward as she circled him with her warm, supple fingers. "We can't do any more for Riley tonight, and I don't want to be alone." Her fingers tightened around him and slid to the base of his shaft. "Make love to me. Make me forget, if only for now. Tomorrow we'll find Riley."

Chapter Eleven

Grace leaned her head back as Declan brushed his lips across hers and then blazed a path along her cheek and down the long line of her neck to the base.

Her pulse beat hard and fast as he flicked his tongue across her collarbone, sweeping the straps of her nightgown over her shoulders and down her arms.

She shrugged, letting the slippery fabric slide farther downward, stopping as it caught on the swells of her breasts. She wanted to be free of the gown, free of all clothing, exposed to his tongue, fingers and any other part of his body that might come into contact with hers.

Her core tightened and a rush of hot liquid slicked her channel in anticipation of what would come.

She leaned into him, wrapped her arms around his neck and guided his mouth lower, toward her aching breasts. She wanted him to take them, to roll the nipples between his teeth, to tongue their tight little buds until she squirmed.

He didn't disappoint. As he trailed his lips lower, she inhaled, raising her chest, offering him more in the movement.

He covered one taut nipple with his mouth through the fabric and tongued the tip.

Grace moaned and circled his leg with her thigh. Pressing her belly to the thick, straining shaft between them.

One coarse hand tugged on the nightgown, dragging it over first one swell and then the other. Free of the speed bumps, the gown drifted to the floor, pooling around her ankles.

Declan cupped her breasts as if weighing them in the palms of his hands. Then he took one into his mouth and sucked, pulling hard, drawing a gasp from her lips.

He let go and lifted his head, a frown descending across his brow. "Did I hurt you?"

She shook her head, barely able to draw air into her lungs. "No," she said. "Don't stop." Grace guided his head back to where he'd been, desperate to again feel the sensations he'd elicited. Her blood hummed through her veins, and heat spread from her center all the way out to her fingertips. She wanted this stranger more than she wanted to breathe.

Declan took the other breast between his lips and tongued, sucked and flicked the nipple until Grace writhed beneath his touch. How could something feel so good but not be enough? She wanted more.

When he raised his head, Declan's gaze bore into hers. "I want you, Grace. All of you."

"Nothing's stopping you," she said, her voice barely above a whisper, her lungs unable to fill with air when he touched her like he did.

He cupped her butt cheeks and lifted her onto the bed, letting her legs dangle over the side.

Grace reached for his jeans, pushing them over his hips.

He grabbed her hands and stayed her action. "Not yet. First I want you to be as crazy as you're making me."

"Trust me," she said. "I already am."

"Sweetheart, you aren't nearly there. I have a lot more I want to do before I come inside you."

Her breath caught and held in her chest and her channel creamed. He had her so turned on, for the moment, she was able to think about him and not Riley.

Declan ran his hands along the insides of her thighs, gripped her knees and spread her legs wide.

Grace's heart raced and her breathing grew ragged.

She reached for his hips, wanting him inside her. Now.

He captured her hands and turned them palms upward, placing a kiss into each palm before letting go. "I want to take you there first."

"I'm already on fire," she assured him.

"Then we'll take it up a notch to incendiary." His lips quirked as he dropped to his knees between her legs.

"Oh, sweet heaven," Grace whispered.

Declan parted her folds with his thumbs and chuckled. His warm breath against her nubbin of desire nearly sent her over the edge. Nearly. Not quite.

A flick of his tongue made her gasp. Another flick got the blood raging, hot like molten lava, pushing through her veins.

Grace threaded her hands through his hair and held him there. "Please," she keened.

"Please what?" he asked and then flicked the nubbin with the tip of his tongue.

"That!" she said, her breathing compromised by the assault on her control.

"This?" he asked and flicked her again, followed by a long sweep and twirl of that incredible tongue.

"Oh, yes," she cried. "That. Do it. Do it again." She let go of his hair and leaned back on her hands, spreading her legs wider. He couldn't get close enough. She had to have so much more of what he was doing to her.

As he flicked that strip of nerve-packed flesh, Declan also thumbed her entrance and dipped into the drenched channel.

Grace shot over the edge, rocketing out to the stratosphere. Her hips rocked and she clutched his head like a lifeline to keep her grounded.

Declan milked her release until her rocking slowed, then he rose between her legs, pressed his shaft to her opening and paused.

"What are you waiting for?" Grace pushed up on her elbows. "Don't you want to make love to me?"

"More than you can imagine. But we need what we found in Riley's nightstand."

Reason returned in a flash. Grace reached beneath her bed pillow and extracted the condom she'd placed there before walking out of her bedroom, dressed in her sexiest nightgown. She hadn't been completely convinced Declan would make a move on her, but she'd wanted to be prepared if he had.

And thank the stars, he had made that move. Never before had she had such a complete and utterly satisfying reaction as she had at Declan's hands...and tongue. Even her ex-husband hadn't been able to elicit such a response. Far from satiated, she wasn't done. She knew he could bring her even more pleasure.

She held up the condom for a moment and then tore it open, rolled it down over his straining shaft and clutched his buttocks. "Please don't make me wait any longer."

He pressed the tip of his shaft against her entrance, barely dipping in and out.

Her control slipping, Grace tightened her hold on his cheeks and slammed him home.

Declan drove deep, filling her, stretching her channel deliciously.

Grace lifted her knees, dug her heels into the mattress and raised her hips, meeting Declan thrust for thrust.

He powered in and out of her, settling into a fast, smooth rhythm, increasing the speed and intensity with each pass.

Again, Grace felt the tingling begin at her center and flood outward, vibrating through her body to the very tips of her fingers and toes. She dug her fingernails into his flesh, urging him to join her in her release.

His body tensed and his thrusts became more powerful until he finally buried himself inside her as deeply as he could go and held steady, his shaft pulsing inside her.

When at last she could breathe again, Grace slowly drifted back to earth and the mattress.

Declan dropped down on top of her, his body limp, his erection still thick and hard inside of her. He rolled them both onto their sides, without losing that intimate connection. For a long moment, he held her in his arms, the silence between them comforting, not awkward.

Grace closed her eyes and snuggled her cheek against his chest. She inhaled the musky scent of his aftershave and sighed. This was what she'd been missing in her marriage.

Pure, unchecked passion.

Declan had it in spades.

Grace realized, from that day forward, she would refuse to accept anything less. She wanted more than just doing it every Friday night on schedule.

Declan had seen to her needs and desires before he'd slaked his own. He gave a damn whether she was satisfied. Her ex-husband hadn't cared enough about her sexual preferences.

She lay in the comfort of Declan's arms and wished she could be there for much more than just the one night.

The truth was that once they found Riley, Declan would be on to his next assignment. After only one day with the man, Grace knew he'd be leaving a new and gaping hole in her love life. More of a hole than the five years with her ex-husband had created.

She must have fallen asleep because the next thing she realized was that something was buzzing and she couldn't seem to wake enough to figure out how to make it stop. She pushed against a solid wall of muscles and sat up in bed, blinking her eyes to clear the sleep from them. At last, she was able to locate the source of the buzzing and lifted her cell phone.

She didn't recognize the number, but figured anyone who called her that late at night might be in an emergency situation.

Or it could be Riley.

She hit the talk button and held the phone to her ear. "Hello?"

"Did he find my file?" Riley's voice came over the cell phone.

"Riley." Grace clutched the phone like a lifeline. "Where are you? Are you all right?"

"I'm okay. But I can't talk long. Did the guy who broke into our apartment find my file box?"

"How did you know about the break-in?" Grace asked.

"It doesn't matter," Riley said. "Did he find my file box?"

"No. Declan scared him off before he got to your bedroom. We found a key in your bank file."

"Oh, sweet heaven. Good. Take that key to the bank tomorrow and remove the contents of my safe-deposit box. I'll contact you tomorrow. Don't tell anyone what you have. If possible, disguise yourself before going into the bank. They're probably already watching you."

"They? They who?" Grace wanted to know.

"I don't know. That's the problem. Get to the bank, retrieve the envelope in my safe-deposit box and hang on to it until I contact you. It's important. The sooner I get it to the right people, the sooner I can come home."

"Riley, what's happening?" Grace asked.

"Sweetie, I'm sorry you got dragged into this. Please stay safe."

"Where are you?" Grace asked. "Let me come get you."

The line was dead…and the call ended. Riley was gone.

Tears welled in Grace's eyes and slipped down her cheeks. "Oh, Riley, what's happening?"

Declan's arms circled her and pulled her back against his rock-solid chest. He held her while the tears fell, comforting her in the darkness.

When her tears were spent, she turned in his arms and rested her palm against his cheek. "Thank you for being here. I don't know what I'd have done without you."

He kissed her forehead and the tip of her nose. "You'd have been just fine."

"Maybe so, but I don't have to be alone. Not when you're here." She pressed her lips to his in a gentle kiss.

He cupped the back of her head and deepened the kiss, his tongue thrusting past her teeth to caress the length of hers.

When the kiss ended, he continued to hold

her, demanding nothing but giving all the comfort she needed.

If only Riley was safe and back in her home, where she belonged, perhaps life could return to normal.

Who was she trying to kid?

Nothing would be the same again, not after having experienced a night in Declan's arms.

DECLAN HELD RILEY close as she slipped into a deep sleep, her breathing steady, her body relaxed against his. If he were any kind of a gentleman, he'd leave the bed, tuck Grace in and go sleep on the couch. But he wasn't, and he didn't want to leave her alone for a second. Not only for her sake, but because of his own desires. He was a selfish bastard.

How, in less than two days, had he fallen completely under this woman's spell?

He'd been homeless, jobless and pretty hopeless before he'd met Grace and Charlie. Now he had an amazing woman in his arms and a problem he had to solve before he could prove to this woman, his family, his new boss and mostly himself that he was worthy of all that had fallen into his lap.

Getting to the bank and removing whatever it was Riley had in her safe-deposit box would be easy enough, as long as the people who'd been after Riley and whatever it was she wanted them to get weren't lying in wait to snatch the item, Riley or Grace. He was pretty sure he could handle one or two attackers, but any more than that would be risky. And he didn't want to risk the lives of Grace or Riley.

His arm tightened around Grace's naked body and his shaft hardened instantly. Though he wanted to make love to her again, he knew how much she needed her sleep.

Smoothing a hand across her brow, Declan tucked a strand of her golden-blond hair back behind her ear. Then he brushed his lips across hers. They were so soft and kissable.

He fought to control the rise of passion, which was threatening to overwhelm him.

With all the strength he could muster, Declan settled back in the bed, closed his eyes and willed himself to sleep.

Dreams came to him of that small village in Afghanistan.

CHILDREN PLAYED IN the dirt in front of their mud-and-stick homes.

He and his team had been to the village earlier that day on a mission to build goodwill between the tribal elders and the American troops that were stationed nearby. They'd also been in the village, scouting for potential infiltrators. The intel community had sent word that the village was harboring a high-powered Taliban leader in their midst.

On that day, Declan and his team hadn't seen any sign of the Taliban, only poor villagers, consisting of women, old men and children. They'd even given the children packets of MREs and a handful of candy.

The mothers had looked on with tentative smiles and softly spoken words of thanks in Dari, one of the official languages of the country.

Later that evening, back at Camp Shorab, the team played cards and joked around before turning in.

Bored of cards, Declan had risen and started for his quarters when word had come from a runner.

"The CO wants you in the ops center ASAP," the young private said.

"Just me?" Declan had asked.

"You and your team," the private had said.

"Coming," Declan said. He hurried back to the card game. "We've been summoned."

The team split, heading to their respective quarters, where they jumped into their uniform trousers and shrugged on jackets. In less than five minutes, they were on their way to the operations center for a briefing on their next assignment.

As he entered the tactical operations center, Declan frowned. His commander stood at the front of the room, along with a brigadier general and four other men. Three of the four men were wearing dark clothes, radio headsets and shoulder holsters with SIG Sauer handguns; they also carried M4A1 rifles with military-grade SOPMOD upgrades. The man speaking with the brigadier general wore a pair of trousers from a business suit, a white button-down shirt, a loosened tie and a bulletproof vest over all of it.

Declan got a bad feeling about the meeting. He shot a glance toward Mack Balkman, his assistant team leader.

Mack shrugged and turned to Frank "Mustang" Ford, their point man who'd arrived ahead of them. "What's going on?"

Mustang shook his head. "I got here a minute before you. They haven't spoken a word to me. I think they're waiting for all six of us to assemble."

Gus Walsh, their radio operator, had arrived at the same time as Declan and Mack. "Who's the dude in the suit?"

Cole McCastlain stepped through the door in time to catch Gus's question. He stared at the man in the bulletproof vest. "I don't know, but he's bound to be important if he comes with his own bodyguards."

Jack Snow, their slack man and the most junior member of the team, entered, buttoning his jacket. "What did I miss?" He stared at the man in the suit and his jaw dropped. "Damn, that's Congressman Patrick Ryan. What's he doing here?"

Declan and the other four members of the Force Recon team stared at Snow.

"How do you know that's Patrick Ryan?" Declan asked.

"Haven't you been following the news? He's been over here for the past couple of days, visiting troops and taking stock of the continued operations in this country." Snow frowned. "Midterm elections are coming." He tipped his head toward the man. "He's probably trying to boost his ratings."

At that moment, the congressman, brigadier general and their commander stopped talking and turned to face the team.

Their commander nodded. "Good. You're all here. Take a seat, gentlemen."

Declan didn't like how formal the CO was. They usually stood around the map and discussed the missions. Apparently, this one would be different. They'd sit and the commander would give them their marching orders. With a brigadier general and a congressman in attendance, their input might not be appreciated.

"Intel had a confirmed sighting of Abdul Kareem Rasul, a high-powered leader of the Taliban's secret organization, the Quetta Shura. He's responsible for the recent attacks on four government outposts in Northern and Eastern Afghanistan, killing thirty-five Afghan security-force guards and four American soldiers. He directed the attack on the hotel in Kabul that killed twenty-two people, including four Americans. He's also behind the bombing of the girls' high school in Logar Province near Kabul. We've been looking for him for three years, but he's been slippery, hiding in the hills and crossing into Pakistan."

General Thomas stepped forward. "Our intelligence operatives tell us he's in the village of Bawshi."

"We were there today and didn't see any sign of him," Declan said.

The general nodded. "Our sources say he's very careful to keep a low profile when he enters a village. They also say he has relatives in the village, which led them to look for him there."

"The point is," Colonel Felton said, "he's there now. Your team is to take him out, using whatever means of force you have available. He's considered dangerous and has already been the cause of many deaths, both Afghani and American."

"We need you to take this man out," General Thomas echoed. "No matter the cost. We cannot let him escape us this time."

Declan nodded. "We'll do our best."

"Do better than your best," Congressman Ryan said. "We've got a lot riding on this operation."

"We'll leave you to the details," General Thomas said and left the room with Ryan and the congressman's entourage.

Colonel Felton waited until the door closed behind them. "You will be equipped with helmet cameras. We'll be monitoring the events as they unfold."

"Great. So, we need to keep our noses clean and kill this guy at the same time." Declan knew the stakes. With the general and the congressman involved, they would be expecting footage to take back to the States to prove their worth on the other side of the ocean. All while he and his men were supposed to go into hostile situations with their hands basically tied. Collateral damage got more airtime than Taliban takedowns.

"Just do your job and don't let Rasul get away," Colonel Felton said.

The team studied the map the intelligence guys had provided with a building identified as Rasul's last known location in the village. They were to go in under the cover of night and take him out with the cameras on to record the event.

Declan had known in his gut that the mission would be difficult. A small village full of women, children and old men would be hard to navigate without civilian casualties. Images of the small children they'd met that day came back to him.

He hardened his heart and got down to the task of planning where they would enter the village, what weapons they would carry and the communications equipment they would need.

That night, the 160th Night Stalkers transported them in a US Army Black Hawk helicopter to within two miles of the village. From there, they hiked the rest of the way, carrying what they needed on their backs, strapped to their chests or in their arms.

As team leader, Declan sported the helmet camcorder.

Mustang, on point, slipped into the village first, keeping them abreast of what he was seeing as he entered. Declan followed, providing cover for Mustang.

At the corner of the next building, Mustang paused.

Declan held up his fist, motioning for the others to hold in place.

"Light ahead. Some kind of gathering. The buildings to my right and left appear empty. Going in."

Declan hurried to the corner where Mustang crouched.

When he reached it, he peered around, his rifle pointed toward the center of the village. As Mustang had indicated, light illuminated the village center, where a gathering had amassed.

"Going to get closer," Mustang said. He leapfrogged to the next mud-and-stick building and stopped.

Declan aimed at the village center, his gaze panning the surrounding buildings and rooftops for any sign of snipers or Taliban gunmen.

At the center of the village, it appeared as though every villager, and possibly more individuals who weren't from the village, were in attendance of some kind of celebration.

Torches had been lit at the village center, casting light and shadows over the men in the headdresses, women cloaked in scarves and children scrambling in and out of the crowd, chasing each other when it was well past their bedtimes.

"I see Rasul," Mustang said excitedly. "He's at the center of the crowd."

Gus, the radio operator, slid in beside Declan. "What have we got?"

"Some kind of celebration," Declan said. "I'm moving forward, cover me."

Gus leaned around the corner of the building, his rifle at the ready. "Go."

Declan hunkered low and ran toward the position where Mustang crouched.

"I don't know, boss," he said. "Doesn't look like a Taliban indoctrination session. Too many women and children in attendance."

Declan studied the crowd. About that time, the people moved, opening a gap so that they could see into the center.

Like Mustang had said, Rasul was there, his bearded face and black turban undeniably distinct. Others around him wore white turbans and next to him stood a young man with a white turban. A woman stood beside the man in white, covered from head to toe in white. Her face could not be seen, but she carried a bouquet of bright red and pink flowers.

"Hell, it's a wedding," Declan declared. "They're having a wedding."

"The general told us to use whatever means we had to in order to take out Rasul," Mustang reminded him.

"Yeah, but storming a wedding would be political suicide," Mack, Declan's assistant leader, said.

"What should we do?" Gus asked into Declan's headset.

Declan shook his head. What could they do? If they didn't take out Rasul, he would live on to kill again. If they raided the wedding party, there would be too many civilian casualties…women, children, maybe even the bride and groom. Despite his commanding officers' orders, he chose to err on caution.

"We wait and see if we can pick off Rasul without taking out the wedding party."

He positioned his men around the village, hoping at least one of them would get a clear shot of the Taliban leader. In the process, they located the vehicles the Taliban had arrived in, parked beneath a crude lean-to with a grass-thatched roof. If they tried to make a run for it, they'd head in that direction.

The celebration went on for another hour, the Taliban leader in the thick of the crowd, too close to innocent women, the bride and groom, and small children. At one point, he even lifted a child into his arms and held her long enough for her to fall asleep on his shoulder.

He was surrounded by other men dressed in white garments, with black turbans. They carried AK-47 rifles and remained close to the Taliban leader throughout the ceremony.

An hour and a half of waiting came to a close when the bride and groom stood and moved toward the Taliban leader. He rose, but was surrounded immediately by women, children and his bodyguards.

"Mack, can you get a clear shot?" Declan asked.

Mack was the best shot among the team. He had logged the highest number of enemy kills in the eight months they'd been in the country. If anyone could take out the Taliban leader, he was the guy.

Mack swore into his mic. "Can't without taking out the bride or groom."

Declan lifted his rifle to his shoulder and aimed at the Taliban leader.

A woman carrying an infant blocked his direct shot to Rasul.

"Anyone else got a direct line of fire?" Declan asked.

One by one, each member of his team reported. "No."

"We have to make a move. If it means breaking up the party, so be it."

"The commander and general both said to use whatever means necessary. You heard them. Rasul has to go," Mack repeated.

"Then let's get this party started." Declan shifted his rifle in his arms. "Be ready. If you get the shot, take it. Do your best to limit collateral damage."

Declan didn't wait for his team to respond; he stepped out in the open and fired his rifle into the air, sure to aim with enough trajectory to take the bullets far from the village. As soon as he fired the burst of rounds, he ducked back behind the cover of the building.

Screams sounded from the crowd and people scattered in all directions. Declan couldn't reemerge from the same building. The enemy would have spotted him and be aiming for him.

Mustang had climbed to the top of the building with his rifle. "I got a bead on Rasul."

"Take him out," Declan said.

"Damn," Mustang said.

"What?"

"He grabbed the bride. He's using her as a human shield." Mustang cursed again. "I can't get a clean shot."

The commander had been clear. He'd authorized using whatever means necessary. In Declan's world, that meant the needs of the many outweighed the needs of the one. One bride.

He could end the terror and destruction of many more by taking the shot…through the bride to the Taliban leader.

"This mission is headed for the crapper," Mack said.

Declan peered around the corner of the building.

The Taliban men had gathered around their leader, holding women and children in front of them. Over the heads of their hostages, they fired their weapons in Declan's direction.

Chunks of hard-packed earth and sticks

splintered off the building beside Declan's head. He slipped back out of range.

He rounded the other side of the building and ran to the next. If he was correct, the Taliban leader and his bodyguards would be heading for their vehicles, which were parked at the north end of the village. They'd have to let go of their hostages long enough to climb into their trucks and SUVs. "Cut them off where they parked," he said.

"On it," Gus responded.

"Getting there," Mack said.

"Almost there," Cole chimed in.

"Right behind you," Snow said.

"Gotcha covered," Mustang added.

Weaving through the narrow streets of the village, Declan came out at the north end, within twenty yards of the Taliban vehicles.

At that moment, it seemed the entire village spilled out of the alleys between the buildings, flowing like a river, carrying the Taliban leader toward the waiting vehicles. He still had the bride clutched against him.

The bodyguards hadn't emerged from the town, which made Declan pause. "Rasul is still surrounded. Where are his bodyguards?"

"Got one coming up from behind you," Mustang said. Shots were fired in the darkness. "One down. Five more to go."

"I'm going for Rasul," Declan said. He started out of the cover of the building he'd been hunkered down behind.

"Hold on," Mustang's voice came across. "We've got a big problem headed our way."

"What?" Declan didn't want to wait too long, or else Rasul would escape, but he ducked between two huts.

"The other five bodyguards are converging on your location. They have babies strapped to their chests and they're herding small children and women through the streets wearing vests full of explosives."

"Holy sh—" Declan cursed beneath his breath. He knew how badly their CO and the general wanted this kill, but to do it would mean taking out the entire village. The face of the child he'd played with earlier swam before his eyes. And then he saw that child emerge in front of the parade of villagers destined to die if the Americans didn't back off.

"Abort," Declan said.

"Abort?" Mack asked. "But we haven't taken out Rasul."

"And if we do, his bodyguards will kill every last person in this village." Declan couldn't live with that on his conscience. If that wasn't bad enough, the press would get hold of the story and blame the Americans. They'd be labeled baby killers, and the corpses of the bride and groom would be paraded in front of the cameras for the entire world to see and know the US Marines were no better than the jihadist suicide bombers who killed indiscriminately.

"You heard me," Declan said. "Abort."

"What about our orders?"

"To hell with our orders. Those people aren't collateral damage," Declan said. "They're people who didn't ask to be used as human shields."

"We're following your lead. If you say we're out of here, we're out of here," Mack said.

The team pulled back, slipping out of the village and into the night to meet up with their ride home aboard the Black Hawk helicopter, their mission a failure.

The next day, Rasul went on to bomb a convoy containing members of the US State Department and a high-powered member of the EU in front of a school filled with Afghan children. Twenty-seven people died that day.

Those in Washington who had authorized the mission to assassinate Rasul were blamed. Heads rolled and the buck stopped with the Force Recon team. Declan and his team didn't know that night they decided not to kill Rasul was the end of their careers as Force Recon marines.

Chapter Twelve

Grace woke to a repeated buzzing. She rolled over and snuggled into the hard, muscular chest beside her and reveled in how safe and warm she felt. She'd never been more content…if not for that annoying buzzing sound.

The man beside her stretched to the side and ended the buzzing, but started talking, pulling her more completely from the deep sleep she'd needed so badly.

"They are?" Declan said. "Yes, ma'am… Charlie. We'll be there in thirty minutes."

Grace opened her eyes, memories of making love to this stranger rushing back to warm her all over. That's when she realized she was still naked beneath the sheets, with her body pressed against his equally naked form.

A different kind of heat rushed into her cheeks. How did she extricate herself from this man gracefully? A man as ruggedly handsome as Declan had to have been with beautiful women in his past. Surely he'd forget her as soon as he completed his assignment and moved on.

Declan started to toss the bedsheet aside, but Grace held on tightly to her corner.

"You go ahead. I'm not quite awake yet," she said, her cheeks so hot she feared she might ignite the sheets. She looked away as he shifted in the bed.

A warm hand caressed her cheek. "Hey, you're not having regrets, are you?" He turned her to face him. Declan leaned up on his elbow and stared down into her eyes. "Because I don't regret a single moment with you. Except…"

Grace braced herself.

"Except that I didn't make love to you sooner." He bent and pressed a kiss to her lips. "You're amazing."

She let go of the breath she held and laughed nervously. "Yeah, but we barely know each other and we're…we're…"

"Perfect in bed together? Fit like we belong together?"

"We're naked," she gushed out.

Declan chuckled. "Yes, we are." He traced a finger along her jaw. "And I'd make love to you all over again, but I don't have enough time to do it right."

"Like you did last night?" Her heart beat like a snare drum, because damn, he'd rocked her world the night before. So much so, she was completely out of her depth and slightly off-kilter. Waking up in this man's arms would be all too easy to get used to. Something she couldn't risk.

Declan wasn't going to be around for long.

The man had a job. She and Riley were that job. When he resolved the problem, he wouldn't have an excuse to hang around. He'd be off to his next assignment.

Would it be a beautiful woman? Would he find her more attractive and a better lover?

Grace bunched her hands into fists, her fingernails digging into her palms, the sting of jealousy burning in her chest. How could she be jealous of a woman who might not even exist? All over a man she'd met the day before.

Again, he cupped her cheek and smiled down at her. "No use being shy. It shouldn't matter after what we shared last night."

"Maybe it doesn't matter to you," she argued, pulling the sheet up over her chest as she propped herself up on her knees. "But it does to me."

He kissed her full on the lips and gave her naked bottom a playful smack. "Then I'll get a quick shower, while you're dressing." He nibbled behind her ear. "Although, I'd rather see your naked body."

He rose from the bed and crossed to the bathroom, magnificently nude, his hips narrow and his buttocks tight and rounded.

Grace couldn't look away. The man was too gloriously good-looking, like a buffed-up Greek god. He shot a wicked smile over his shoulder. "Caught ya looking."

Again, her cheeks heated. She grabbed a pillow and threw it at his head, the sheet she'd held to her front slipping to expose a breast. She quickly covered herself. "You're way too full of yourself, Declan O'Neill."

He smiled and winked. "Maybe, but you still looked." Declan entered the bathroom and soon the sound of water hitting the shower curtain came through the paneled door.

Grace sprang from the bed and pulled on her robe, knotting its tie securely. She was grabbing her clothing and shoes when Declan emerged from the bathroom, a towel slung low around his hips. He wore nothing else.

Grace's jaw dropped and she ran her tongue across her suddenly dry lips. "Uh, my turn in the bathroom?"

He nodded. "Yes. And I would have dressed first, but my bag is out here."

She started around him, but he hooked her arm as she passed and slid his hand up to hers, where she clutched her clothes to her chest as if they were armor.

"Do I make you nervous?" he asked, a frown drawing his eyebrows together. Declan lifted her hand to his lips and pressed a kiss to her palm.

She stared at his mouth, rather than his eyes. "I'm not ready for this," she whispered.

"For what?"

"You know…" She should have pulled her hand free, but she couldn't. His fingers on hers, his lips on her skin… "I'm not ready to jump back into the morning-after routine.

I don't know how to date. I don't remember how to act after…well…after…"

He gathered her in his arms and held her. "Maybe we shouldn't have gone so fast, but I can't regret what happened last night. My only regret is that you're uncomfortable now." He leaned back, tipped her chin up with his finger. "Would it make you feel better if we can pretend it didn't happen and go back to friends working to find Riley?"

As much as she'd like their connection to be more, she really wasn't ready for it. Her heart beat too fast and her knees wobbled. Both symptoms could be attributed to the fact she was pressed against his naked body, the electricity generated scrambling her brain.

"Yes," she said.

He brushed his lips across hers in barely a kiss, then he straightened and stepped away.

Grace dove for the bathroom, shut the door, threw her clothes on its hook and leaned against the wall. She didn't want to go back to being friends, not after experiencing the magic of a night in Declan's arms. But she wasn't ready for the pain and disillusionment of being discarded once the magic wore off. Three years after her divorce, she had just begun to feel right in her own skin. Her ex-husband had been so controlling and critical of everything she did, she had to fight her way back to any level of confidence. She couldn't afford to lose that.

She pushed away from the wall, leaned over the sink, splashed water onto her face and then brushed her teeth. She noticed a red mark on her neck where Declan's stubble had rubbed against her skin as he'd kissed his way down to her breasts. Her nipples puckered and tingled at the memory of his tongue flicking the tips.

With a groan, she splashed cold water on her face again and patted it dry, refusing to acknowledge the red marks or pointed beads of her nipples making little tents against her robe. No, she couldn't go there. Riley was her focus.

Hoping it would calm her down, she took a fast shower, toweled off and ran a brush through her still-damp hair. She pulled on her clothes—just jeans and a soft blouse—ready to face the day...and Declan.

When she exited the bathroom, she entered the empty bedroom. Through the open bedroom door, she could see Declan standing in the living room, at the boarded-up window.

He turned when she approached. "My team has arrived at Mrs. Halverson's. The bank doesn't open until nine o'clock. I'd like to swing by Charlie's place and connect with them before we hit the safe-deposit box. I think they will be useful in providing backup when we retrieve whatever Riley stashed there."

"I'm all for additional protection. I'm afraid whatever we're getting from that safe-deposit box would either hurt who she's running from or is something they want."

"Exactly." Declan's brow dipped low on his forehead. "Which puts you in just as much danger as Riley's in now."

A shiver rippled down the back of Grace's neck.

"Are you okay with this? You could hand the key over to the FBI and give them permission to enter that box."

Grace shook her head. "I can do this. Once I have it, she'll contact me for the handoff. She said not to trust anyone."

"Not even me?" He gave her a gentle smile that made butterflies take flight in her belly.

"I trust you," she said. "You saved Mrs. Halverson from kidnappers. You went after the intruder in our apartment. I'm convinced you would have done both those things regardless of who Mrs. Halverson was."

He shrugged. "I did what any decent human would have done."

Grace chuckled. "Most people would have saved themselves and never considered going after the bad guys." She stared up into his eyes. "You're real hero material."

"Not according to the US Army." His lips thinned into a straight line. "If you're ready, let's go."

She hoped Declan would loosen up enough to tell her what he'd done that got him discharged from the military.

A few moments later, she settled into her SUV, stealing a glance over to where Declan sat with his hand curled around the steering wheel. Trusting him was not an issue. Grace trusted the man with her life. She just wasn't sure she could trust him with her heart.

DECLAN PULLED THROUGH the gate at Mrs. Halverson's estate in Kalorama twenty minutes later. A dark SUV stood in the circular drive.

His pulse quickened and his heart grew

lighter as he climbed out of the vehicle and rounded to the passenger door.

Grace had the door open and was swinging her legs out.

He extended a hand and helped her to her feet, then tucked her arm through his elbow and led her up the stone staircase to the front double-door entrance.

Before he could reach for the bell, the door burst open and five men spilled out.

"O'Neill," Mack greeted him first with an outstretched hand.

Declan grabbed his assistant team leader's hand and tugged hard, pulling him into a tight hug and then clapping him on the back.

"You're a sight for sore eyes," Mack said.

"Good to see you, man." Declan's eyes stung. He knew he'd missed his team, but hadn't realized just how much. Now that they were in front of him, he felt as if he'd come home.

Mustang nudged Mack aside and moved

in for a bone-crunching bear hug that left
Declan chuckling and breathless. "Missed
you, old man." Mustang stepped back and let
Cole, Gus and Jack have their turns at greeting their old team leader.

"Who do you have with you?" Jack held
out his hand. "I'm Jack Snow, slack man on
the team."

"Grace Lawrence." Grace's brow wrinkled.
"What's a slack man?"

"He's the newest man on the team," Gus
said.

"Which makes him the pack mule," Cole
added. "He carries everything the rest of us
don't want to carry." He backhanded Snow in
the belly. "Speaking of which, where'd you
put my duffel bag?"

"Bite me," Snow said. "We're not on active duty anymore. You carried your own bag.
Find it yourself."

"We're a team, aren't we?" Cole said. "Every

Force Recon team needs its slack man. If you're not our slack man, what are you?"

"Excuse these two jokers." Mack pushed Cole and Snow aside. "I'm Mack Balkman, assistant team leader, second only to our man O'Neill." He held out his hand to Grace.

Cole and Gus introduced themselves to Grace, each holding her hand a little longer than the last.

Finally, Declan had enough and walked between Gus and Grace, forcing Gus to let go. "When did you get in?" Declan asked.

Gus grinned and stepped back.

"I got in around two in the morning," Mack said. "Snow came in shortly after me."

"Gus, Mustang and I came in around two in the morning, too. We drove in from Virginia Beach," Cole said.

"Becoming professional beach bums?" Declan asked. "You haven't gone soft on me, have you? I sold you to Charlie as the best of the best."

"Yeah, but you didn't tell her the best of what, did you?" Mustang winked.

"We're ready and more than willing to do whatever you have in mind," Cole said. "A couple of months of hanging out at the beach and going to the bar was getting old." He cracked his knuckles. "I'm ready to get back into the action."

"You mentioned using our skills," Mack said. "What exactly do you and Charlie have in mind?"

Declan waved toward the door. "Let's go inside and I'll brief you and Charlie on what's going on."

An hour later, Declan's team had been briefed and had come up with a plan to support Grace on her trip to the safe-deposit box at the bank.

"It might be overkill," Mack said.

"But better overkill than mission failure or Miss Lawrence getting hurt," Charlie said.

"I'm glad you're all going with her. I'd go my-self, but that might add more complications to the operation. Especially after what hap-pened the other day."

"True." Declan wouldn't want to worry about two women at the same time, especially one who'd proven to be a target for kidnap-pers. He didn't like the idea of Grace putting herself into danger, but she insisted she had to do this for Riley.

"I'm leaning toward overkill," Grace said. "I'll feel a whole lot better with a few more able-bodied men watching my back. With your help, I'm going to walk into that bank, get whatever is in that safe-deposit box and walk back out." She wiped her hands together. "That's it. No problem."

A knot formed in Declan's gut. His instinct told him it wasn't going to be that easy. Some-one had killed Moretti. If the killer wanted what Riley had stashed in that box, he might be willing to kill Grace to get it.

"If you don't mind, I like the redundancy of having my team as backup. I'm hoping it's as easy as you seem to think it will be. If it is, great. If it isn't, we have skilled operatives who know how to take the bad guys down."

Grace gave Declan a twitch of a smile. "I'm okay with your way of thinking. It's almost time for the bank to open," Grace said with a glance at her watch. "Let's go."

"Wait." Declan held out his hand. "Give me your cell phone."

Grace's eyes narrowed. "Why?" she asked as she handed it over to him.

"Just in case, for some unexplainable reason, we get separated, I want to be able to find you." His gaze captured hers. "Do you mind if I put a tracker on your phone?"

She shook her head; her heart was warming to the idea. He cared enough to want to find her should they be parted. Sure, it was all because of the task he'd been assigned, but she liked that he would go to the trouble to set it up.

He brought up the applications store and selected a tracking application. When it had downloaded, he added information that would allow his cell phone to track hers. He handed the phone back to her and she put it into her pocket.

"I'd rather tag you with a smaller tracking device, but for now, this is what we have to work with."

Charlie stepped up beside them. "Declan, you and I need to work on what our new organization might need in the way of communications equipment and weapons."

He nodded. "And we will. But for now, we have to get moving."

Declan insisted on leading the way out to Grace's SUV. He helped her into the passenger side and slipped in behind the steering wheel.

Mrs. Halverson had loaned the men two

of her estate's black Cadillac Escalades. The men split up, two in one vehicle, three in the other. They could all have fit into one, but this way they had multiple vehicles if they needed to chase the bad guys.

Charlie stood beside the lead vehicle as the men climbed in. "I took the liberty of loading the rear of these with some of the weapons my husband collected in his own personal armory. Hopefully you won't need them. But I also included ammunition, should things get sticky. If this weaponry gets you in hot water, call me. I know people who will make sure authorities know you're okayed to use these things."

Declan bent and kissed the older woman's cheek. "Thank you. It's nice to know you're looking out for us."

The drive to the bank took fifteen minutes. Declan pulled the SUV into the parking lot beside the one-story, gray stucco building.

Grace didn't say a word on the way. She sat

with her gaze on the road ahead, her purse clutched so tightly to her chest, her knuckles turned white.

Declan reached over and touched her hand. "You'll be all right."

She gave a shaky laugh. "I don't know how you and your team could walk into enemy territory and not be scared out of your minds."

"Don't let my team tell you differently," Declan said. "We were pretty scared at times. We just didn't let it slow us down. We had a job to do, and got busy doing it. The end usually justified the means, and we did our best to make our efforts count."

Declan slowed at an intersection and then turned right. "Until we didn't follow orders," he added softly, his lips pressing together.

"You must have had a good reason." Grace tilted her head and stared into Declan's eyes. "If you had it all to do over again, would you have made the same decision?"

An image of the babies strapped to the Taliban's chests and the bride and groom being used as human shields flashed before Declan's mind. "Yes."

"Then you did the right thing." Grace smiled. "Now, let's get this over with. I want my roommate back in one piece. Preferably alive." She faced forward, her head held high.

Declan's lips twitched.

Grace was scared, but she would do whatever she had to in order to help her friend.

Declan parked as close to the front entrance as possible.

When Grace started to get out, he put up a hand. "Wait for me. I can't protect you if you're standing out in the open, alone."

She stared at him. "As long as you don't intend to use yourself as a shield to catch bullets aimed at me."

He shrugged. "I'll do what I have to. Hopefully it won't come to that."

Grace frowned. "It better not. I like you just the way you are. Not peppered with lead."

She chuckled. "I never thought I'd utter that phrase. Sounds like something out of an old Western movie."

The other members of his team arrived shortly after Declan and Grace, parking at opposite ends of the lot, probably trying to look like they weren't arriving together.

When they got out of the SUVs, they were so much alike in build and bearing, only an idiot wouldn't put the five of them together.

Declan preferred that they act as a visual deterrent to anyone who might try to attack Grace. He glanced around the lot. Several cars were parked and two more pulled in as he helped Grace down from the vehicle. He slipped an arm around her, pulling her as near to his body as possible.

She didn't resist; instead, she leaned into him, holding her purse in front of her. "You think anyone will try to attack me?"

"I don't know. But I don't want to take any chances." He smiled down at her. "I think I like you, and would hate for anything to happen to you so early in our potential relationship."

She shot a quick glance up at him. "You like me?"

He nodded with a gentle smile. "Yes, I do. So, let's get this over with so we can have coffee and get to know each other in a little-less-volatile environment."

"I'm game." She smiled up at him and walked with him to the door.

Once inside, Declan loosened his hold but didn't relax his vigilance.

Grace asked to access the safe-deposit box, showed her identification, along with the power-of-attorney papers, and presented the key. The receptionist asked them to take a seat and left her desk to find a manager. She was gone for at least five minutes when finally a dark-haired man appeared with a smile, wearing a name tag with Branch Manager engraved on the gold-colored metal. He introduced himself as Alan Jordan. He checked the computer, presumably looking up the box information. After he verified Grace was who she said she was, he finally showed her into the vault where the boxes were located.

When Declan went to follow, Jordan held up his hand. "I'm sorry, sir, only the key owner is allowed into the safe."

Declan was forced to remain outside the safe until Grace returned. He didn't like it, but he couldn't argue against the rules.

The entire time he waited, he studied the people coming in and out of the bank.

An old woman walked in with a cane, her body hunched over, her gait slow and steady.

A man wearing jeans and a polo shirt came in, carrying a money bag for deposit. He nodded toward Declan and headed straight for the tellers' counter.

Mack and Gus entered without giving Declan so much as a nod. They made brief eye contact and stopped at the receptionist's desk to inquire about opening accounts.

A woman carrying a small baby came through the doors and stood in line at the tellers' counter, bouncing the baby on her hip as she waited.

None of the people in the bank appeared to pose a threat to Grace.

Declan checked his watch. Grace had been inside for three minutes. How long did it take to open a safe-deposit box? He paced the floor in front of the receptionist's desk. The woman had yet to return to her post. Had she gone on break?

He looked around at the different offices, all with glass fronts and people working with customers. The receptionist had gone down a hallway to an office that didn't have glass walls.

Declan assumed the office belonged to the branch manager. Until that moment, he hadn't thought about why the receptionist hadn't come out of the branch manager's office with him, assuming she might have gone on break in the back of the building.

Not wanting to leave his position in front of the vault, Declan nodded toward Mack, who was waiting in a chair for an account representative to call him to open an account.

Declan caught Mack's gaze and tipped his head in the direction the receptionist had gone.

Mack rose from his chair and walked toward the hallway.

One of the loan officers chose that moment to enter the hallway ahead of Mack and knocked on the closed door.

When she didn't get a response, she opened the door and leaned in. The scream she emitted echoed throughout the bank lobby, generating more screams from the tellers and account representatives.

The loan officer raced back toward the lobby and ran into Mack. When he caught her shoulders, she screamed again and struggled to get free. "They're dead. Oh, my God. Laura and Mr. Jordan are dead!" She collapsed against Mack.

Declan leaped over the counter and ran toward the safe, his heart pounding hard against his ribs.

If the receptionist and Mr. Jordan were dead, who was the man in the vault with Grace?

Chapter Thirteen

Grace walked into the vault with the branch manager, clutching the key to the safe-deposit box in her hand. This was the day of reckoning. Riley must have stored something very important in the box. In Grace's way of thinking, it could be a life-or-death revelation.

Her mouth dry and her heart racing, Grace followed Mr. Jordan into the room with the safe-deposit boxes. He searched the numbers until he found the one that matched the key she held. "This is the one. You'll need to use the key to open the box."

"Could I have a moment alone?" Grace

asked. She didn't want the bank manager to see whatever it was she was supposed to retrieve from the box. Not knowing what it was, she wasn't sure anyone else should know.

The man's smiled slipped. "I'm sorry, Miss Lawrence, a bank employee has to witness the removal of anything from the safe-deposit boxes. If you don't mind, I have work to do. Could you hurry it along?"

Grace frowned at the man's rudeness, but she got on with the reason she'd come to the bank in the first place. Riley wanted her to get something out of the box. If she was that concerned about retrieving the item, it had to be important.

Her hand shaking, Grace slipped the key into the lock and turned it.

Mr. Jordan stepped up beside her. "Here, let me help you."

"That won't be necessary. I can manage on my own." She gripped the handle and pulled the drawer out of the wall of boxes far enough so she could reach inside.

The box was high up the wall, so Grace couldn't look down into it. She pulled it out and set it on a table in the center of the room for this purpose. Nothing was inside the drawer except an envelope, which she quickly retrieved.

Clutching the envelope in her hand, Grace slid the drawer back into the wall of safe-deposit boxes and removed her key. "I'm finished here. I'm ready to go." She turned to leave.

A hand wrapped around her face, covering her mouth.

Grace tried to scream, but the hand clamped tighter, muffling her attempt.

"Give me the envelope," Mr. Jordan said, his voice hard and steely, not at all like the accommodating manager who'd shown her into the vault.

An icy shiver ran from the base of Grace's

skull all the way down her back. Using one of her self-defense moves, she twisted free of Mr. Jordan's hold and turned to face the bank manager, a frown pulling her eyebrows together.

"You heard me." He held a wicked-looking knife in his right hand and motioned with the left. "Hand it over."

Grace shook her head, her fingers curling around the envelope. "But it's just a piece of paper." With something small and square inside. And Riley needed it. "Why would you want something so personal?"

"Your roommate has been duping us for the past few months. It's time she gave us what we paid good money to acquire."

"I don't know what you're talking about."

"You don't need to know. Just hand over the envelope." He grabbed her wrist in a vise-like hold.

Using the self-defense techniques she'd learned from a police officer at the local

YMCA, Grace twisted her arm and thrust it downward and out, breaking the man's hold.

He swung the knife at her, catching her sleeve, the tip nicking her upper arm.

Grace eased backward toward the vault door. "You're not the branch manager, are you?" One step at a time, she edged toward the exit, still holding the envelope in her hand.

"Give me the damn envelope," he demanded and lunged.

Grace screamed and dove for the door, and she would have made it out, but the man with the knife was fast and had longer legs. He threw himself at her, tackling her like a pro football player.

Grace hit the marble-tiled floor hard, the air knocked from her lungs.

"Give me the envelope," he said, his voice low and dangerous. "Or I'll slice into your jugular."

"It's mine," Grace cried and kicked at the man's hold on her ankle.

He let go long enough for Grace to jerk her leg free and scramble to her feet.

She made it all the way to the threshold of the vault before he caught her by the hair and yanked her back against him.

He pressed a knife to her throat and growled into her ear. "Make any stupid moves, and you won't see your precious roommate ever again." He pressed the tip of the knife into her skin.

Sharp pain made Grace freeze. She didn't dare scream again for fear the man would carry through on his promise. "Take the envelope," she said, lifting it up for him to grab.

"I will," he said. "But you're coming with me as collateral. I know your boyfriend has this place surrounded with his buddies. They won't let me out of here unless I take out a little insurance policy." He let go of her hair and wrapped his arm around her middle, still pressing the knife to her throat. A warm, wet trickle dribbled down Grace's neck.

With her heart racing and her knees shaking, she struggled to keep her wits about her, searching for any opportunity that might present itself to make an escape. If her abductor would just not press the tip of the knife so hard into her skin.

From behind, he walked her through the vault door and nearly ran into Declan.

"Get back!" the man behind her yelled. "Get back or I kill the girl."

Declan raised his hands. "Okay, okay. Don't hurt the woman." He eased backward. "Let her go and I promise you won't be harmed."

The man snorted. "I'm not letting go of my little insurance policy. She's coming with me. Now, move out of my way or I stick it to her." He increased the pressure on the knife and more blood trickled down Grace's neck.

"All right. Calm down." Declan's nostrils flared and he stepped to the side. "Just don't hurt her. We'll give you whatever you want."

"That's more like it." Grace's captor half

lifted, half shoved her forward. "Tell your men to stand down." He kept moving forward. "Now!"

Declan raised his voice, "Mack, Gus, stand down."

Grace couldn't turn her head left or right to see Declan's guys, but no one came running to help her. And she was glad they didn't. If the hand at her throat tightened any more, that knife would slice right through her jugular vein and she'd bleed out before they could call 911.

She kind of liked her jugular vein intact. "I'll be okay," she tried to assure Declan, though she had no idea how she could possibly be fine. The man would have no more use for her once he got away from the bank and claimed whatever was in the envelope Riley had asked Grace to retrieve.

"That's right," her abductor said. "Play your cards right and I'll let your girlfriend go when I'm well away from here." He squeezed his arm hard around her middle. "Call the police, and I'll take her apart, one piece at a time."

Declan's fists clenched and he took a step forward.

Her captor faced him with Grace between the two of them. "Don't think I will?" His voice deepened to a low, dangerous growl. "Try me. Maybe I'll take her pretty ear first." He trailed the knife up to her ear.

Grace closed her eyes and gritted her teeth, prepared for the pain sure to come.

"No need. I believe you," Declan said.

Grace opened her eyes and stared into Declan's.

"I'll get you out of this," he promised.

She gave him a weak smile. "I'm counting on it." Her eyes stung with unshed tears. She couldn't see how he would be able to help her. Until the man holding the knife put down his arm, she was his to toy with, to threaten and use as a shield.

"I'll need a car and a fifteen-minute head

start." Her captor returned the knife to the base of Grace's neck, where her pulse beat a thousand times a minute. "If all goes well, you'll see your girl again. If not, well, it's on you. Make sure I get out of here, and I'll go easy on her."

Grace doubted the man would keep his word, but she didn't have much of a choice. She'd have to go with him unless she found an opportunity to run before he got her into his car. She braced herself, ready to react at the slightest chance she might get away.

DECLAN COULD HAVE kicked himself. How had the man gotten into the bank before Declan and his guys? The only way he could have done it was if he'd had prior knowledge that Grace had found the key and was going to the bank. Perhaps he had tapped Grace's apartment or had some way of listening in on her conversations with Riley or Declan. However he'd done it, the fact was he had Grace and would use her to extricate himself from the bank and from any confrontation with the police.

Declan had failed Grace and now had to find a way to get her out of the danger she faced. He'd been on fire with worry when he'd heard her scream for help earlier.

"Let me go ahead of you to let my guys know you're coming out." Declan hurried to the lobby doors and stepped outside. He spotted Snow and Mustang standing at the corners of the building and Cole leaning against an SUV, pretending to talk on his cell phone.

When they saw Declan, all three men straightened.

"Grace is coming out. She's not alone, but don't make any sudden moves." He stood back and held the door. "My guys won't get in your way," he assured the man holding Grace.

The man led Grace through the door, his eyes narrowed, the wickedly sharp, military-grade knife firmly pressed to Grace's throat.

If Declan dove for the man's arm, he might be able to knock the knife loose. Or he might bump the man's hand and be responsible for the knife slicing into Grace's jugular vein. He couldn't take that risk. The thought of anyone slicing into Grace's long beautiful neck made his stomach roil.

He couldn't take a shot at the man for fear of hitting Grace, or missing and the man following through on his promise to slice her throat.

Declan couldn't do a damned thing but let the man go…with Grace.

The abductor walked with Grace into the parking lot, turning again and again, his gaze on Declan's men, his lip pulled back in a feral snarl, daring them to make a move.

Each time Grace faced Declan, he died a little more. The man was getting away with the woman Declan felt could change his life for the better. She was everything he could have wanted in a woman and more. So beautiful, inside and out. He couldn't let it end here. He wouldn't.

A car whipped around the end of a row of parked vehicles and drove up beside Grace and her captor. The passenger door was flung open from the inside.

Still holding the knife to Grace's throat, the man backed into the seat, forcing Grace to sit on his lap, blocking any chance for anyone else to get a bead on him and blow him away.

A moment later, the car burned rubber, speeding out of the parking lot.

And Declan's heart slipped like a bag of rocks to the pit of his belly.

Grace was gone.

His men gathered around him.

"We can't just let him get away with her," Mack said.

"If we go after them, he'll know and kill her," Cole reasoned.

"Now that he's gotten away, what's to keep

him from killing her anyway and tossing her body out in a ditch?" Mustang said.

Declan shot a murderous glare in his teammate's direction. "He's not going to kill her. And we don't have to follow closely. I have her phone on a tracker."

"What if he finds her phone on her and he tosses it out of the vehicle?" Gus asked.

"Then we're sunk." Declan punched the code into his phone to find Grace. When the screen came up, he could see that the phone was still moving. "For now, she still has it." He ran toward Grace's SUV. "Let's move."

Before they could get out of the parking lot, a plain silver sedan pulled in and blocked the exit. A woman with auburn hair leaped out and waved them down. "Any of you Declan O'Neill?" she asked.

Declan shifted into Park and flung open his door. "I am."

"I'm Riley." She glanced around. "Where's

Grace? Did she get the envelope out of my safe-deposit box?"

"She did." Declan's jaw tightened. "And someone got her and the envelope."

Riley swore beneath her breath. "I should have gotten it myself." She glanced around. "I can't stay out in the open. Where can we go to talk?"

"Get in the car. We were about to follow the tracker on Grace's phone."

"Thank God." Riley pulled her car to the side and jumped in with Declan.

He handed her the phone with the tracker. "Navigate. We have to catch up before they discover her phone on her."

Riley shook her head. "They're not going to be happy with the memory card they have."

"That's what was in the box?" Declan asked. "A memory card?"

"A very small memory card, packed with the data they wanted all along."

"What the hell's going on? Why have you

been on the run? And why do they want this card?" Declan wanted all the information he could get. Grace's life was on the line, and the more he knew about his adversaries, the better equipped he'd be to face them.

"I'm working on a secret project. I can't tell you exactly what it's about, but I can tell you that I was approached by the FBI to help them find out who was stealing secrets from Quest about this particular work. I didn't know how to do it other than to create two sets of data. One good set and one bad set. I presented the bad set. It was the one that was being sold to whoever was buying. I figured I'd keep putting out the bad data until we found the culprit." She stared out the window. "I didn't think it would take so long for the seller to surface. And I never considered it would put Grace in danger. I thought I was the only one committing to the undercover sting."

"Did you figure out who was selling the data?"

She glanced his way. "I think Moretti was in on it. But I didn't think he was smart enough to orchestrate the deals. Someone with a better understanding of what this idea is worth has to be behind it. Someone with connections to foreign buyers." She shook her head. "Moretti isn't that guy. He doesn't like traveling outside the region, much less the country. Oh, he was involved, but I think he was just a middle man. He took the fall for someone else."

"Any idea who?" Declan asked.

Again, Riley shook her head. "I was getting close to finishing the project with the good data and knew I wouldn't be able to hold out much longer. The program team was at the point they needed my work to complete the project. It was key to making it all work."

"I take it whoever was buying the bad data figured out it was bad."

Riley nodded. "I got a text just as I got to my office two days ago. The message said to get out." She pressed a hand to her chest. "I've never been so scared in my life. I got up from my chair, grabbed my purse and walked out of the office, out of the building and kept walking. Another text told me to lie low, find a hotel, but pay cash. In other words, I had to disappear. I couldn't even call Grace to let her know what was happening." Riley sighed. "Until I bought a burner phone."

"Were you the one who warned us to get out of the bar?"

She nodded. "I didn't know if they'd come looking for me at my apartment. If they did, they'd find Grace. So I've been shadowing her since this all began, staying far enough away to remain in hiding, but close enough to warn or help out, if I could. I was meeting with my FBI handler this morning when you and Grace were on your way to the bank. I left that meeting as soon as I could. I never thought anyone would dare to cause trouble at a bank. Outside the bank, maybe, but not inside a bank." Riley banged her fist against her palm. "I should have gotten the key from Grace and gone into the vault myself. I didn't even tell the FBI handler about the spare memory card. I was afraid a double agent might be working against me."

The road they followed led toward Baltimore. Soon they were passing through a warehouse district and shipyards where cargo and containers were stacked neatly on the shore.

"Is the memory card Grace retrieved encrypted?" Declan asked.

"Yes," Riley said. "They won't be able to break into the data. We don't have to worry about them getting into the information."

"You might want to revisit that idea. If they can't get into that information, they might kill Grace out of anger."

Riley shot a fierce frown in his direction. "Damn." She glanced at the screen, her eyes widening. "The cell phone locator blinked off." She looked up.

"Damn," Declan echoed. "Without the locator, it will be impossible to find her. She could end up anywhere."

Chapter Fourteen

Grace sat stiffly in her captor's lap all the way through the city, scared as much by the knife at her throat as by the DC traffic and her lack of a seat belt. Darkened windows kept anyone from seeing her inside during snarled traffic. There was no way she could signal someone for help.

She braced a hand on the dash and prayed they didn't hit anyone in front of them or were hit from behind, thus throwing her through the windshield.

Eventually, they broke out of DC proper

and headed toward the warehouses and docks near Baltimore, MD.

All the while, Grace prayed Declan and his guys would catch up and do something to help her out of the situation.

At the very least, she hoped the police would stop them for having two people in the passenger seat, neither in a seat belt—if they could see in. What happened to stopping people for not wearing seat belts? Why did stuff like that never happen when you needed it to?

Neither Declan nor the police caught up to them. And if they had, Grace was sure the driver would have made a run for it, thus initiating a high-speed chase that would have ended badly for more than just the people in the car she was in. Others on the highways would have suffered. Her only saving grace was that they hadn't found the cell phone she'd tucked into her jacket pocket.

She waited patiently for the car to stop and

her captor to get tired of holding her and put down his knife.

When they'd come to a long line of container yards at a shipping port, her captor finally lowered his knife.

Grace inched her hand toward the door handle, waited until they slowed at a corner and then yanked, shoved the door open with her foot and tried to dive out.

The arm around her middle caught her before she could clear the door, and dragged her back inside the vehicle.

After bringing the car to a screeching halt, the driver grabbed her hair and pulled hard enough to bring tears to her eyes. He held her by her hair until her abductor could close the door again.

The man holding her around her waist shifted her around, settling her back in his lap. In the process, he must have felt the phone in her pocket. He swore and dug it out. He rolled the window down, cocked his arm and almost threw it out. But he must have thought better of it, pulled the back off and removed the battery instead. He dropped it into his pocket and retrieved his knife, pressing it to her throat again.

The driver released her hair, returning his hands to the steering wheel.

Grace's heart sank to her knees. She'd hoped Declan could track her phone, but with the battery removed, he wouldn't be able to.

Resuming his course, the driver continued past several yards before he pulled into one. He weaved his way through to a small office nestled in the middle of rows and rows of stacked containers in all colors and markings.

Once the vehicle stopped, several men in dark clothes stepped out of the little office building, carrying semiautomatic weapons or handguns.

One of them approached the passenger door and opened it.

Her captor shoved her off his lap and into the arms of the man who'd opened the door.

Grace ducked her head and plowed into the man's belly, hitting him as hard as she could.

He grunted and doubled over.

Grace used that opportunity to slip past him.

She didn't get far before he snatched her wrist and yanked her backward. He spun her around, twisted her arm up behind her back and applied enough pressure that Grace was forced to stand on her toes to keep the pain at bay.

The man who'd kidnapped her got out of the vehicle and stretched.

Grace still held the envelope she'd retrieved from the bank. She tried to slip it beneath her shirt, but her captor caught her wrist before she could and ripped it from her fingers.

"The boss has been waiting for this." He turned and walked toward the office building.

"What do you want me to do with her?" the

man holding her arm up between her shoulder blades asked.

"Throw her in one of the containers or kill her," her captor said. "I don't care."

Grace's heart leaped into her throat and her pulse hammered against her eardrums. She couldn't let them kill her. She had too much to live for. Riley would be beside herself, and Declan…

Grace wanted to get to know the marine better. She knew in her bones the man was special and that he would be worth the effort to live, if only to see him once again. He'd given her hope that not all men were like her ex-husband.

Her original captor paused in front of the structure. "No, wait. Don't kill her. We might need her again. But go ahead and lock her in one of the containers."

The man holding her grunted his acknowledgment and shoved her toward a row of the long, rectangular boxes.

He opened one with his free hand and swung the door just wide enough for a person to fit through. Then he ratcheted her arm up a little higher in the middle of her back.

Grace couldn't get any higher on her toes to relieve the pressure. Tears burned the backs of her eyelids. She bit down hard on her tongue to keep from crying out or showing any fear.

The man shoved her hard from behind, sending her flying into the container.

She fell, landing on her hands and knees. Before she could scramble to her feet, the door slammed shut behind her, leaving her in the dark, dank, steel space.

She felt her way along the sides to the door and ran her hand all along the interior, searching for a lever or latch that would allow her to open her cell. She couldn't find one.

Knowing the containers sometimes had doors on both ends, she felt her way along the side to the other end and again searched for a handle, lever or latch.

Hope leached from her system when she realized she was trapped inside the metal box, with no way to get herself out. She leaned against a wall and slid down until she sat. She couldn't lose her confidence now. Declan would find her. She had to believe that. He'd promised she'd be all right. All she had to do was wait and reflect on all that had happened in the past forty-eight hours.

She'd gone from worrying about finding a full-time job to worrying about living to see another day.

If she lived, she hoped and prayed her roommate was alive and well and found a way out of the danger she was in. On a more selfish note, Grace hoped she'd get to spend more time with the hunky marine. He was a man worth getting to know. A man a girl could count on when times were tough. A man of integrity and honor.

What couldn't have been fifteen minutes later, the metal-on-metal sound of the latch being moved on the door made Grace lurch to her feet. The door to the container swung open.

Her captor stood outside with a gun pointed at her chest. "Come with me."

Unless she wanted to risk having a massive hole blown through her, Grace had no other choice. She marched at gunpoint into the little office a few yards away, grateful to be out of the metal box.

Inside the office, several men gathered around a computer monitor. One sat in a dilapidated office chair, his fingers flying feverishly over the computer keyboard. He cursed and slammed his hand on the metal desk. "She's got it encrypted and password protected. It could take me days to hack in."

"We don't have days. We have to know that we can access the data. The boss is already angry he doesn't have the correct information. He will not be pleased if we leave here without what we promised. We might not live long enough to hack in." The man who was speaking turned to Grace.

She studied his face with all the intention of picking him out of a lineup, if the need arose.

He had short, dark hair and brown-black eyes. Thick eyebrows practically grew together over the bridge of his nose. He wore black trousers and a black jacket. His eyes narrowed as he studied her. "You will enter the password for this memory card."

Grace shook her head. "I don't know it."

He pressed a handgun to her temple. "Enter the password or die."

Grace had been through a lot that day. Having another weapon pointed at her should have made her shake in fear, but somehow she was beginning to get used to it, or she was numbing to the danger. She shrugged. "I guess you'll have to shoot me. The only person who knows how to get into that memory card isn't in this room." She lifted her chin and focused on not flinching if the man pulled the trigger. If she was going to die, she'd die fearless. On the outside, if not inside.

She waited, fully expecting the gun to go off and her life to end.

When it didn't, she flashed a glance at the man. He lowered his handgun and turned to the man who'd disguised himself as the bank manager. "You said she had a cell phone. Give it to me." He held out his hand.

Grace's original captor dug the phone from his pocket and handed it to the dark-haired, dark-eyed man, who quickly reassembled the battery and replaced the back. When the phone had booted, he handed it to Grace. "Call Miss Riley Lansing."

Grace shook her head. "You won't get the code to get in. I know my roommate. She would never betray her country by selling secrets."

The man snorted. "Let's test that theory. Call her."

"No," Grace said.

Red flooded the man's ruddy cheeks and his eyes narrowed even more to a squint. He grabbed Grace's hand and bent her thumb back so hard, she was convinced it would break. The pain had her twisting and writhing.

"Are you going to call your roommate? Or am I going to break each of your fingers, one at a time?"

Grace gasped. "I'll do it." Feeling as if she was failing her friend, she placed the call, praying Declan and his buddies had some way of finding her soon. She didn't want to put her friend in danger, but calling her might buy Grace time for the men to get to her first.

She pressed the last number with which she'd had contact with her roommate.

I'm sorry, Riley.

As THEY NEARED the location where the cell phone had stopped moving, Riley's burner phone rang.

Declan nearly drove off the road in an attempt to reach for it. He righted the vehicle and focused on staying between the ditches.

Riley punched the button and held the phone to her ear, her gaze on Declan's. She listened for a moment and nodded. "Don't hurt my friend. I'll do whatever you want. Just don't hurt her."

Declan's chest tightened. He wanted to reach through Riley's phone and choke the person on the other end of the conversation. If anything happened to Grace, he'd personally hunt down anyone who harmed her, and kill them with his bare hands.

Riley's frown deepened. "If you hurt her in any way, you can forget about getting into that data. I'm the only one who knows the password for that file. Look, I'll make a deal with you. You trade her, unharmed, for me. When I see she's well away and safe, I'll give you the password and you can have it all. Just tell me where to meet you." She paused. "I'll arrive unarmed and alone." She paused again and then continued, "How do I know you'll release my friend? I'm not just going to walk into a trap and give you all the cards to hold."

It was making Declan crazy to hear only one side of the conversation. Sitting back and listening wasn't the action he needed to unleash his pent-up energy.

When Riley ended the call, she stared down at the handheld device. "At least they're willing to make a trade." She sighed. "I knew I shouldn't have agreed to work with the FBI. None of this would be happening. I'd be blissfully ignorant that I was aiding the sale of secrets to foreign spies. And Grace wouldn't be held hostage by ruthless thugs."

"You did what you thought was right," Declan said softly. Doing the right thing didn't always work out well in the end. Much like what had happened to himself and his team. The corners of his lips twitched. "No good deed goes unpunished. We will get Grace out of this alive, if it's the last thing I do."

"We might get that opportunity to rescue her. Only I have to go in alone." Riley's lips thinned and she stared at the road ahead. "Though I have to go in alone, it doesn't mean you and your men have to wait for Grace to come out. You can be infiltrating the area all around our rendezvous site. You just can't let them see you." She turned to face him. "We need to nail these bastards. Not only are they threatening my best friend, they're stealing secrets from our country."

His fingers tightened on the steering wheel as he pictured Grace being led off by the man with the knife to her throat. She had to still be alive. He wanted so much more time with the woman, having only scratched the surface of her personality and desires. "Grace was willing to do anything to find you. She's amazingly loyal and determined."

Riley's brow dented in the middle as she studied him. "You like her, don't you?"

Heat rose in his cheeks. "She's an amazing woman," he said, refusing to look toward his passenger lest she see how deeply his feelings were entangled in the pretty blonde's life.

Riley's brows rose. "Oh my God, you two had sex?"

His foot jerked off the accelerator for a moment. "Who said we had sex?" Making love to Grace after such a short amount of time together sounded insane. But they had. And it had been incredible, soul-lifting, life-affirming and Declan wanted to do it again. But he didn't want the world to know. Not yet. He didn't want anything or anyone intruding on his campaign to win over the sexy divorcee.

Riley frowned. "You didn't take advantage of her, did you?"

"No. I would never take advantage of Grace. She deserves nothing but happiness."

"I agree. But what are your intentions toward her?" Riley insisted.

"I have to state them now, even though we only met a little over a day ago?"

"Hell, yeah. Grace is my best friend. We look out for each other."

"Even though you keep secrets from her?" Declan asked.

"You know the government rules," Riley said. "Top secret means you don't even tell the ones you love. I love Grace like the sister I never had. She is my sister in my heart. She deserves to live and be happy."

Declan didn't know what the secrets were that Riley couldn't reveal, but he knew enough about Grace to know she could be the one for him. He needed more time with her. Maybe the remainder of his life. In the few hours he'd known her, he'd come to care for the woman. He'd wade through a field full of enemy snipers to free her from the bad guys.

"I agree. Grace deserves to be happy and live a long life."

"I'm glad you feel that way." Riley gave him a lopsided smile. "Her ex-husband didn't give a damn if Grace was happy as long as she made his life more comfortable and entertained his guests exactly the way he liked."

Declan's jaw hardened. "Sounds like a winner."

"He's a real jerk, and he did a number on my friend. I'm glad Grace got away from him. She's come a long way in regaining her confidence." Riley poked a finger at Declan. "Don't screw it up."

Raising his right hand, Declan nodded solemnly. "I'll do my best to make it right for Grace."

"Good. Because if you don't, you'll have to contend with me."

He nodded. "Understood." Hauling in a deep breath, he let it out slowly and then clapped his hands. "Let's go get Grace," Declan said. "But first we need a plan." He motioned for his team to pull into an empty parking lot. They all exited their vehicles and gathered around their team leader.

Declan briefed them on how they would let Riley drive into the meeting alone, but not until the team had infiltrated the location and were ready to take action.

"We have only a few minutes' lead on Riley's expected arrival. We have to make good use of that time." Declan went to the rear of one of the Escalades and opened the back. Inside was a large plastic box containing military-grade rifles with high-powered scopes.

"It's a shame Charlie's husband is dead." Mack lifted one of the rifles out of the box and held it in his hands. "I think I would have liked him."

"He had good taste in weaponry." Gus selected an AR-15 rifle with a scope and grabbed a magazine full of rounds. He slammed the magazine into the weapon and slipped the strap over his shoulder.

Cole did the same and selected a nine-millimeter handgun, as well.

While his men armed themselves, Declan looked up the meeting location on a map application on his smartphone. They were less than a mile away. After each of Declan's team members secured a weapon and loaded it with ammunition, they synchronized their watches and took off on foot to the site. Riley would wait for fifteen minutes and then take Grace's SUV to the rendezvous location.

By the time she arrived, Declan would have his men in place.

As they reached the edge of the container yard, clouds moved in, darkening the sky and signaling a storm. Declan had the men fan out and move in, keeping a close watch out for Tangos in sniper positions atop the containers. They moved from shadow to shadow on silent feet, their urban-operations training coming back to them.

Though they didn't have the high-tech communication devices they were used to as Force Recon marines, they had their cell phones and Bluetooth earbuds to keep in touch while moving through the container yard. Before they'd entered the yard, Declan set up a conference call with all of his team, Riley included. They left the call up as they moved in.

When he and Charlie had time, he'd make sure his team had the best communications equipment and weapons. If they were going to take on tasks like the one that had presented itself in Grace and Riley, he would make sure they had the tools to be successful no matter what the assignment.

"I'm headed your way," Riley said into his earbud at the fifteen-minute mark. "ETA three minutes."

"We'll be ready," he said softly.

Mustang had point, moving through the

containers ahead of the rest of the team. "I see a small office building in the middle of these building blocks," he reported.

"Any Tangos?" Declan asked.

"None so far." Mustang paused. "No, wait. I see one on top of a container near the office structure."

"Don't take him out until the rest of us get in place. We can't spook them until the exchange of hostages is underway."

"Roger," Mustang said. "I'll be ready. In the meantime, you can move forward. The other guards are on foot on the ground, near the office. I count five." He gave their locations. "Going silent. Getting too close for chatter."

Declan and the other four members of his team slipped between containers, hugging the shadows.

Gus, Cole and Snow circled around to where Mustang had indicated three of the guards were standing at the corners of the metal shipping containers.

"Bear in mind, if bullets start flying, it's possible some will ricochet off the metal," Mack warned.

Declan heard the words, but his attention was now on the office building he was almost certain held the woman he'd come to save.

No sooner did he have it in sight than Grace's SUV appeared from around a corner of containers stacked three-deep.

"Everyone in place?" Declan asked.

One by one his men checked in, careful to be quiet and not walk on each other's transmissions.

When all had reported in, Declan slipped through the increasing darkness of the murky sky, edging toward the office.

Riley pulled in, stopping short fifty yards away from the building. She sat in the SUV for a long time without opening the door.

Declan could imagine the woman working up the nerve to get out and expose herself to being shot at or nabbed before they let Grace go free.

The office door opened and four men surrounded a tall man with black hair and dark eyes. He held Grace in front of him with a handgun pressed to her temple.

His rifle tucked into his shoulder, Declan stared through the scope at the men surrounding Grace. He didn't have a clear shot yet. They were standing too close to her.

He turned his scope to Grace and his heart skipped several beats.

She walked with her shoulders back and her chin held high. The woman was not going to show those men fear.

Declan's chest swelled with pride at the same time as fear squeezed his gut. Anything could go sideways. Grace was in grave danger.

"Should I get out now?" Riley asked, pulling Declan back to the task at hand.

"No," he said. "Stay until they get far

enough away from the building that they can't run back in."

"Did you forget?" Snow mentioned. "I have a grenade launcher. All I need is a clear shot."

"Hold on to that thought," Declan said. "Hopefully we won't need to destroy the office and everyone in it."

"But if we do, I'm your man," Snow said. "I have the most recent experience with this weapon."

Declan chuckled. "Okay, I'll keep that in mind. Just a reminder, our goal here isn't to blow up buildings. We're here to rescue two women. We are not in the Middle East, and explaining a grenade launcher to local authorities could get sticky."

"Roger," Snow responded. "Although I do miss blowing up stuff. Do you think we'll ever get the chance to level any buildings ever again?"

"Not anytime soon," Declan said.

Snow sighed. "Then I'll just have to make do with my rifle."

"Are you with us, Mustang?" Declan asked into his mic.

"Raring to go," Mustang responded. "What's the first order of business?"

"Be ready to take out the sniper up top," Declan answered. "Make it as quiet as you can."

"I have him in my scope," Mustang whispered.

"Okay, Riley," Declan said. "You can open your door and lean out. Tell them to let Grace go and you'll come to them."

Riley did as Declan said. She opened her door and leaned out. "Let Grace go, and I'll come willingly."

"Get out of the SUV now, or we will shoot your friend."

"If you shoot my friend, I'll run you over with my car. And don't think shooting me will help you. You still need me to open that memory card. So let her go." Riley spoke with iron-hard firmness.

"I think I'm in love," Mack said.

Declan ignored his assistant team leader's comment, his focus on the men standing near Grace. One of them led her forward and slightly in front of him, a handgun pressed to her temple, her arm twisted up behind her back. He stopped in front of the SUV where Riley sat. "Get out of the car," he said. "You won't run me over as long as I have your friend. And if you don't get out, I'll shoot her."

"What do I do?" Riley asked quietly.

"Again, tell them to let her go." Declan couldn't quite get the shot on the man holding Grace close to his chest. "Whatever you do, don't get out of the vehicle."

The man holding Grace moved the gun away from her head and fired a round into the ground. "Get out, now! Or she dies."

Declan jumped. Grace's captor appeared to

be losing his patience. If he'd just move an inch more to his left…

Declan controlled his breathing though his heart raced. He didn't dare open fire until he had a very clear shot. One that didn't involve shooting Grace in the process.

Chapter Fifteen

Grace knew she had only one shot at escape. When the guy holding her shifted his weapon away from her temple, she took her chance. Ignoring the pain in the arm he had jacked up between her shoulder blades, Grace cocked her free arm and slammed her elbow into the man's gut.

He jerked his hand up, firing another round that pierced the front fender of Grace's SUV.

She twisted around, broke free of his grip and dove for the ground, rolling beneath the carriage of her SUV.

Gunfire sounded in the container yard, with

the ping of bullets bouncing off metal storage boxes.

Grace lay low with her hands over the back of her neck. She couldn't tell if the gunfire was all from the men who'd held her captive, or if there were more men in the yard. Based on the number of shots fired, she suspected there were more people firing than just the men responsible for her abduction. She prayed the others were Declan and his team of defenders.

The sound of bullets hitting her car made her afraid for Riley. Her roommate needed to be down lower, out of the line of fire.

Grace inched her way beneath the chassis of the SUV to the driver's side and she poked her head out into the open. The driver's door was open. Riley lay over the seat.

For a moment, Grace was afraid Riley had been hit. "Riley! Sweetie, are you all right?"

"Grace?" Riley started to raise her head.

"Keep low, Riley. Can you get out and onto the ground beneath the SUV? It's probably safer down here."

"I don't know."

More gunfire sounded, making it feel like a war zone.

Grace wasn't giving up. She'd finally found her roommate. She sure as hell wasn't going to let her die from a gunshot wound.

Shouts sounded and footsteps pounded across the pavement.

Grace rolled over and glanced toward the front of the vehicle. The man who'd most recently pointed a gun to her temple lay on the ground in front of the vehicle, a pool of blood forming beside his head.

Usually very forgiving of transgressions, Grace couldn't find it in her heart to forgive any of the men who'd held her hostage that day, or who had broken into her apartment. She hoped they burned in hell.

Again, she turned her attention to Riley.

"Come on, Riley, we need to get to somewhere safe. You have to come down here."

Staying as low as possible, Riley turned in her seat behind the steering wheel and glanced down at Grace. "You don't know how glad I am to see you."

Grace smiled. "I could say the same, but we can't waste time. Come down here and slide under the SUV."

Riley grabbed the keys from the ignition and tossed them to Grace.

Grace caught them and tucked them into her pocket. Then she eased Riley's feet onto the running boards as she slid out of the SUV and to the ground. Once there, Riley dropped all the way down until she lay flat against the pavement. She tucked her arms beneath her and rolled under the chassis.

Grace rolled in beside her roommate and waited for the opportunity to run for the shelter of one of the containers. She low-crawled to the rear of the vehicle and gauged the distance between the SUV and the nearest metal storage box. It might as well have been the span from one wall of the Grand Canyon to the other. To cross it would put them out in the open long enough for a bullet to catch at least one of them.

She turned back to Riley and gasped.

Her roommate slid backward out from beneath the SUV, her fingernails digging into the pavement but finding no purchase.

The man Grace had thought was lying dead in his own pool of blood had a hold of Riley's ankle and he was pulling her out from beneath the SUV.

Grace tucked and rolled toward Riley, determined to get to her before the gunman had a chance to pull her all the way out from beneath the vehicle.

By the time she spiraled out from beneath the car, Grace was too late.

Her captor had Riley in a choke hold around her throat. "Make a move, and I'll kill her."

Grace didn't hesitate; she swept her leg to the side as hard as she could, catching the man in the shin. His legs buckled and he flailed his arms, releasing his hold on Riley.

Riley dove forward, out of the man's reach.

The dark-haired, dark-eyed man hit the ground hard.

Grace scooted back to where Riley sat against the side of the SUV. She gathered her friend in her arms and held her close as the battle raged around her. "I was wrong. Get back into the SUV."

"I can't." Riley shook so hard, her teeth rattled.

"Climb into the vehicle," Grace ordered. "I'm getting you out of here."

Riley rallied, pulled herself up into the SUV and over the console to the passenger side.

Grace had to wait for her to get all the way across before she could climb up. She'd placed her foot on the running board when she heard a shout in the distance and another voice sounded behind her.

"I should have killed you from the start."

Tired to her bones, Grace turned to face the barrel of a handgun.

The man she'd just kicked in the shins held the weapon, standing a little too far away for her to knock it out of his hands or slam the door on his arm. This was it. Her number was up.

What she needed now was a miracle.

DECLAN WAS TOO far away from the action to help Grace when she made her move. As soon as she dove for the ground, Declan fired on the man who'd been holding her. Declan had to trust Grace had gotten out of the line of fire, because as soon as he took the shot, all hell broke loose.

"Get the sniper," he called out to Mustang.

Gunfire rang out.

A man dropped from the corner of a stack

that was three containers high. With the sniper out of the game, they were on a more level playing field. But there were plenty of places to take cover with the heavy metal container boxes to hide behind. The trouble with the boxes was that they didn't absorb all bullets. Some of the rounds ricocheted off the metal sides and continued on to strike other things.

Declan hoped those other things weren't his teammates or the women.

He aimed his weapon at the men near the small office building. They took up covered positions behind other cars in the parking lot and it became an all-out war. Instead of hiding in trenches, they took cover behind vehicles and slung bullets back and forth.

These men weren't regular Joes off the street. They were highly skilled killers with weapons as impressive as Mr. Halverson's collection. "Take your time," he cautioned his team. "Conserve your ammunition. You'll get the chance to take them out when they start making mistakes."

Declan's team knew how to tease them into expending ammunition. They fired enough to keep the enemy firing until the numbers of bullets dwindled.

A shadow moved by the office building.

Declan lined it up in his scope and discovered a man hiding behind a pillar. He kept his sights on the target and waited.

The man held up a rifle and aimed at Declan.

Declan pulled the trigger first. The man fell and lay still against the ground.

That's when he saw Riley being held by the man he thought he'd already killed.

His heart seized in his chest and he shifted his aim. But he couldn't shoot without taking out Riley. Then the man toppled sideways, and Riley dove beneath Grace's SUV.

Declan shifted his attention to the ground

where Grace lay on her side, with her leg out-stretched.

He chuckled.

She'd taken the man down with a sweep of her leg.

Grace and Riley huddled together for a moment on the ground and then Riley climbed into the vehicle.

Good. They could get in and drive away, out of range of any gunmen.

Then he noticed the man Grace had knocked down reach for the handgun he'd dropped.

"Grace, watch out!" he cried. He raised his rifle to his shoulder and stared through the scope, praying his aim would be true and swift.

The man stood with his handgun pointed at Grace.

Declan held his breath and squeezed the trigger.

The sound of his rifle firing seemed to be echoed by the blast of another weapon.

For a long moment, the man holding the gun and Grace remained exactly as they'd been before Declan pulled the trigger.

Then the gunman crumpled to the pavement. A half second later, Grace slipped to the ground, as well.

Declan's heart stopped beating.

"That was the last one down. All bogeys have been accounted for," Mack said into Declan's Bluetooth earbud.

Declan couldn't understand the words over the buzzing in his ears. He staggered to his feet and ran toward the SUV.

"Grace!" he called out, his eyes burning, his heart breaking into a million pieces. He couldn't see her face, couldn't tell if her eyes were open. Had she been injured? Or killed?

He ran as fast as his feet would carry him, sliding down on his knees when he came to a halt in front of Grace.

Her eyes were open. By all that was good in the world, her eyes were open.

Tears stung the backs of his eyelids when he realized she wasn't dead.

"Grace," he said and pulled her into his arms. "Are you hurt? Were you shot? Tell me you're all right. I think I died a thousand deaths in the past thirty seconds." He pushed her to arm's length, his gaze raking over her. "Talk to me."

She laughed and shook her head. "I would, but you wouldn't shut up long enough." Grace smiled up at him. "I'm okay. But after all we'd been through today, and then nearly being shot in the chest, I just couldn't stand anymore." She cupped his cheek. "I'm sorry I scared you, but I was a little scared myself for a while there."

He bracketed her face between his palms and stared into her eyes. "You are the most amazing woman I've ever known. I want to hold you, kiss you and shake you for scaring years off my life." He laughed and pulled her close again. "Promise me something, will ya?" he said against her ear.

She shivered at the way his breath on her neck made her all hot and aware of him as a perfect male specimen. "Promise you what?" she said, her voice ragged, breathy with desire.

"Promise me you won't get cornered by a gunman ever again. I don't think I can handle it."

She smiled and pressed her lips to his. "I'll do my best to keep that kind of promise. Trust me, I don't ever want to be at the business end of a handgun anytime in the rest of my life."

"And promise me, now that we found your friend, you aren't going to disappear out of my life. I think I could fall for a girl who can defend herself and her friend. You're my hero." He kissed the tip of her nose and then brushed her lips with his.

"Are you kidding? I'd be dead right now if you hadn't taken out that guy. At that precise moment, I was in the market for a miracle, and you came through with it." She wrapped her arms around his neck and pulled him down for a toe-curling, heart-stopping kiss that rocked him to his very core.

When the kiss ended, Declan laughed. "Yes, I think I could very easily fall in love with you."

"Good," she said against his mouth, "because I'm well on my way there myself."

He leaned back, a frown tugging his brow downward. "You'd want to be with a guy who has a dishonorable discharge on his record?"

"Only if it was you. What I've learned about you so far is that you're a straight shooter and you believe in fighting for what's right. Whatever you did to get kicked out had to have been for all the right reasons. I know that in my heart."

"For the record, I didn't follow orders. It meant taking a shot through a bride and a groom on their wedding day and through babies strapped to Taliban cowards." He shook his head. "I refused to shoot through the innocents. A particularly bad terrorist got away because my teammates and I refused a direct order to take out the target no matter what. That refusal, plus a politician's agenda, got us released from military service."

"I'm sure if you had appealed the decision, they would have overturned it," she said.

He shook his head. "It's a done deal. Besides, the guys and I have jobs we can stand behind. We're going to help Charlie fight for truth and what's right."

"And maybe find time to see me?" Grace added. "I'd really like to see you again, even if your assignment is over."

"You can count on that. I might even take you out to dinner and dancing."

"You really know how to sweep a woman off her feet."

Declan pulled her into his arms. "I think you've proven you can sweep a man off his feet. You've blown me away in the short amount of time we've known each other. I look forward to more time with you."

"Do you think you two could break it up long enough to explain to the local police why there are dead men lying around a container yard?" Mack stood over them, shaking his head.

Declan pushed to his feet and reached down to take Grace's hand. "Time to call Charlie. Let's wrap this up. I have a date with a beautiful woman."

He pulled Grace up and into his arms. "I'm glad I found you on that sidewalk in the middle of an attack."

"Me, too," Grace said. "I can't even imagine what might have happened had you not been there that day. If I didn't believe in fate before, I do so now."

Epilogue

Charlie sat at her desk in her Washington, DC, mansion, staring at the men sitting and standing in the massive office. "Now that you have located Miss Lansing, and the people responsible for abducting my new assistant Grace from the bank have all been accounted for and jailed, what should we work on next?"

"We need to ramp up with communications equipment, first thing," Declan said. "And I don't think it's over for Riley Lansing. She seems to think the guy behind the sales won't stop with the death of her supervisor, Moretti."

"Any guesses as to who is behind the sale?" Charlie asked.

Declan shook his head. "No. And since Riley is the only one who can decode the memory card, they will continue to target Miss Lansing until they get what they paid for, regardless of her FBI handlers."

Charlie nodded. "Sounds like we still have a task. We need to provide protection for Miss Lansing." Charlie looked around at the six men in her office. "Anyone here want to take on the responsibility of being a bodyguard to a highly intelligent young engineer?"

Mack stepped forward. "I'll do it."

Declan clapped his friend and second in command on his shoulder. "You've got this. And we'll have your back, should you need us," Declan said. "And my gut tells me you're going to need us."

Mack snorted. "And I thought fighting the Taliban was difficult. I have a feeling Miss Lansing will give me a run for my money."

* * * * *

LET'S TALK

Romance

For exclusive extracts, competitions
and special offers, find us online:

f facebook.com/millsandboon

⊙ @millsandboonuk

🐦 @millsandboon

Or get in touch on 0844 844 1351*

For all the latest titles coming soon,
visit millsandboon.co.uk/nextmonth

*Calls cost 7p per minute plus your phone company's price per
minute access charge